When Will You Quit?

21 Keys to Living The Life God Designed For You

LISA HAROLD

Copyright © 2018 by Empoword Publishing Worldwide
in conjunction with Lisa Harold
When Will You Quit? 21 Keys To Living the Life God Designed For You
by Lisa Harold

Printed in the United States of America. All rights reserved solely by the author. The author guarantees all contents are original and do not infringe upon the legal rights of any other person or work. No part of this book may be reproduced in any form without the permission of the author. The views expressed in this book are not necessarily those of the publisher.

The scanning, uploading, and distribution of this book or any part thereof via the Internet or any other means without the permission of the publisher or author is illegal and punishable by law. Please purchase only authorized editions and do not participate in or encourage the electronic piracy of copyrighted materials.

Acknowledgements

I want to first acknowledge my Lord and Savior, Jesus Christ. It is only through His strength that I was able to write this book.

To my immediate family who've been such a blessing to my life and very instrumental in who I am today. Without your encouragement and support this would not be possible.

To all of my friends and family who believed in me enough to push me pass my limits and wouldn't allow me to give up on my dreams. There are too many names to mention here, but you know who you are, and each one of you is important to me. I could not have been as successful with my life and book as I am without you! Thank you.

Table of Contents

Introduction 1

SECTION ONE: DISCOVER

Chapter 1: Identify Your Past 4

Chapter 2: What Is Purpose? 8

Chapter 3: Roadblocks to Purpose 15

Chapter 4: Know Yourself 22

Chapter 5: Identify Your Strengths 26

Chapter 6: Identify Your Weaknesses 29

Chapter 7: Humility of Purpose 34

SECTION TWO: DEVELOP

Chapter 8: Mindset 41

Chapter 9: Core Habits 46

Chapter 10: Walking in Integrity 50

Chapter 11: Self-Control 55

Chapter 12: Forgiveness 62

Chapter 13: Surrender 67

Chapter 14: Intentional Friendships 72

SECTION THREE: DEPLOY

Chapter 15: Have A Vision 83

Chapter 16: Have A Plan 87

Chapter 17: Conquering Your Fears 91

Chapter 18: Walking in Courage 96

Chapter 19: Strategic Connections 100

Chapter 20: Leaving a Legacy 104

Chapter 21: Commitment 108

Introduction

Due to unfortunate circumstances, as a child, I was placed in many foster homes. I would get comfortable with a family and then be uprooted and placed with another family. This happened year after year until my heart was numb. Because of this I never felt like I belonged anywhere or to anyone. I carried this feeling all of my life. Throughout my adult years it left me asking myself, why am I here? That became my daily prayer. I felt like I simply existed with no purpose at all. Having a great job, and a loving family, still left me feeling unfulfilled. I had bad days, good days, and shared many laughs, but at the end of it all when I laid my head on my pillow, I was lost. I was depressed. I was always frustrated and confused with no direction of what steps I needed to take to change this life of hopelessness. I began to think if this is all life has to offer then what's the point of being here. "There has to be more to life"; became the resounding statement in my mind. I'm sure you have said this many times, if not currently now.

Feeling unfulfilled, I went on a quest to discover who I was and free myself from this seemingly purposeless life. I remember one night, in particular, lying in my bed tossing and turning, restless, feeling discouraged and discontent with life. The discontentment I felt nudged me to sit up, and I noticed a blue light shining through my bedroom blinds. I moved to the edge of my bed, pulled the blinds back to look through and to my surprise it was the moonlight. It was a full moon that night, and the blue light radiated my entire room. As I sat there looking out the window, the beauty of the moonlit sky captivated my empty heart and I began to cry uncontrollably. I looked intently at the moon, and the stars in the sky and in that moment it was as if beauty collided with misery and gave a ray of hope. I heard a soft, gentle voice say, "There is so much more for you." That was a defining moment in my life where I truly began to seek God. I wanted to find out what more could there be for me. I was determined not to quit on this journey until I found out because I knew the life I was living wasn't doing it for me and I needed help.

Over the past 15 years, I've discovered who I am, and how to live life intentionally through discovered purpose. The book you're holding contains keys that I have applied in my own life. These keys have set me free from living a life of existing while being unfulfilled. This book will help you answer many of your unanswered questions, bring clarity to how you got here, and provide direction to move forward with practical tools to unlock your destiny. As you read, you will find new levels of freedom with each chapter. If you feel empty or simply not satisfied due to the belief that your life is unfulfilled, then this book is for you. Let's take this journey to discover the life God designed for you.

Section One:

DISCOVER

Chapter 1
Identify Your Past

Let's get one thing clear: you are *not* your past. Although your past gives insight into who you've become, it does not define who you are. So often we look back at our past as the defining indicator of who we are. Instead, we need to consider how our past has shaped us into who've we've become today.

From the moment you were born, you were being shaped by the words spoken over your life each and every day. Your personal experiences played a major role in shaping who you are today. The behaviors your parents, peers, and other influential people modeled also contributed to the person you are today. Let's not forget how the circumstances and situations you experienced played into making who you are. The person you have become is a collection of the words others have spoken over your life, your personal experiences, behaviors others have displayed for you to follow, and the circumstances, both good and bad, you have lived through.

Although the negative words people use regarding you have the power to shape you or your thinking about yourself, you do not have to accept them as your identity. Just because somebody says something about you doesn't mean that those words are true of who you really are.

You may have had unfavorable personal experiences in your life, but they don't have to define who you truly are. Growing up, you may have been exposed to a bad example of marriage; however, that marriage doesn't mean that's how yours will or should be. Perhaps you have had more than your share of unfortunate circumstances occur in your life. You do not have to let those circumstances determine your identity.

The reality is, we have all developed a certain mindset of our lives based on our past. If you don't recognize the negative factors in your past that have shaped unhealthy mindset and habits, you will live a life God never intended for you to live.

Would you say that bad habits have become a normal part of your life? Is it because you have adopted those bad habits as truth? I want to challenge you to redefine and rediscover what truth is to you. Is it what you've seen and heard in the media? Is it what influential figures in your life have told you or modeled for you? Is it what you've read in a book? No doubt, several contributing factors have influenced how you live your life, which then define what your life is like. But you don't have to embrace them as your truth.

As a child, I loved to laugh. I laughed all the time. One day someone told me that a person who laughs a lot is deceitful. Hearing this declaration from this person who was important to me, I accepted it to be my truth and stopped laughing a lot. I believed that too much laughter, or even smiling too much, couldn't mean anything good. From that day on, unknowingly my laughter turned into sadness. That precious little girl, who was once always so joyous and would light up a room with her smile, didn't want people to think she was deceitful or that something was wrong with her, so she decided to stop laughing and smiling so much. My decision at that moment to embrace those untrue words caused me to shy away from who I really was. It began to shape a life for me that was never mine to live.

Now fast forward to my college days, when I encountered a group of ladies who were just as happy as they could be, always smiling and seemed very excited. They would go around campus talking to other ladies about Jesus. I immediately thought something was wrong with them. In fact, I thought they were on drugs because no one could genuinely be that excited all of the time. Thankfully, the ladies were not on drugs. I, however, believed this to be true at that time, and it was all because I had allowed someone's words to define my truth for me.

People say you never really know how things affect people and it's so true. We never really know the condition of a person, and everyone is affected differently. Things take a toll on your mind and sink deep, and it's hard to break certain patterns of thinking, especially if that's what you've seen for most of your life. You get locked in a closet of false realities that may have started at different times of our lives, mostly beginning in childhood, and then carried into adulthood. It's important for you to identify those factors in your life so you can begin to transform your mind into right thinking. That takes me to, what is your point of reference for which you base your truth on? That question is one of the most important to ask yourself, because how you live your life is based on the answer you give. Sadly, most people's point of reference for truth is nothing more than lies that have been masked as truth. Some of the lies that people will tell you are that you are stupid, dumb, and won't be anything in life. They will make you believe that you are a failure. They will lie to you and convince you that since your parent's marriage ended in divorce, then marriage is not worth fighting for. Perhaps you've seen someone close to you get abused; therefore the lie that tries to become your truth is that you will have to accept abuse in your own life whether its verbally, physically, or sexually. If all you've seen is chaos in your family growing up, it's tempting for you to recognize chaos as normal and the lie tells you to continue those bad, destructive habits. No matter what lies others have spoken to you or even the lies that you may have spoken to yourself, you can make the decision today not to allow those lies to define who you really are. The fact of the matter is, most of the times the people in your life are not intentionally trying to hurt you with words or examples, they just don't understand the impact that their choices have on you. Maybe they had a rough life and are reflecting themselves on you.

My parents had me at a fairly early age. At that time in their life, they made many life choices that affected me tremendously. At the age of three,

I was taken away from my biological parents. I began to grow with a void inside of me and have feelings of not being wanted. It affected my relationships mainly with guys because I wanted to feel wanted and accepted so bad that I sought their attention. I'm saying all this to point out the fact that in spite of the choices that my parents made with their life, I had to make my own choices. What they accepted as their truth, I had to choose whether or not I would allow those same things as my truth. Ultimately, I chose to accept a different truth.

    I'm reminded of a family in the bible. The Bible doesn't tell us much about the husband, Salmon; however, it is very clear that Rahab was a prostitute before becoming married. Salmon and Rahab had a son named Boaz. Boaz would later grow up to become a very wealthy and influential man. He actually became his family's redeemer. Despite the fact that Boaz came from a prostitute, God used him to be a redeemer of his family. God has a specific call on your life regardless of your family's history. Their past, as well as your own past, does not have to dictate the truth about who you really are. You are NOT your past!

Chapter 2
What is Purpose?

Tell me if you agree with this statement: One of the most frustrating things in life is not knowing why you are here. This was something that I personally struggled with for most of my life. I actually dealt with a great deal of depression that I wrestled with until I was about eighteen years old. During that time, I was doing what most people do. Every day, I would wake up and go about this thing we call "life," but inwardly, I felt so empty from the purposeless life I was living. There was a great void in my life. I experienced really great days in my life; however, none of them compared to this dark feeling of being in the world but not feeling like I was alive. It was agonizing. It was a feeling that I thought I would never be able to shake free from.

Nothing I would do helped me escape this feeling of my breath being sucked right out of me. Existing in life this way is a lot like having a sore that you keep picking at. You think that peeling the scab will fix it and get rid of the residue of the scar, but in reality, it only makes things worse. The scar heals, but it doesn't heal properly. Instead, it ends up leaving an uglier scar than before because we did not allow ourselves the power in learning how to heal properly. This is probably the most crippling thing in many of your lives. So how do you know if you are living God's purpose for your life or not? I want to identify some signs that help you understand if you are living God's purpose and give insight into ways you can discover your purpose.

Let's first look at what *purpose* is. Purpose is simply why you were created. It is the intent behind your design. We all have a common purpose, but then we have individual purposes that God creates each of us for. The common purpose that we all share, which is also the big picture of why we were created, is ultimately to bring glory to God here on earth. Can you dare to believe that you were actually born out of purpose? You are a purposed being with flesh on your body. Jeremiah 1:5 reads: "Before I formed you in the womb, I knew you. Before you were born, I set you apart and appointed you a prophet to the nations." This passage is evidence that before we were even formed in our mothers' wombs, God already knew what he placed on the inside of us. He knew the purpose that He wanted us to fill here on earth. God had given Jeremiah the purpose of being a prophet to the nations long before Jeremiah was a baby in his mother's arms. Likewise, every single person on the face of the earth already has a purpose on the inside of him or her. That's right, you already have a purpose on the inside of you. You are not here by accident. It doesn't matter what anyone has said to you about your purpose. God has already created you with purpose on the inside of you according to His word. God took purpose in the palm of his hand and then he placed your flesh around it. You are a purposed being with a fleshly body! This means that you don't have to try and find out what your purpose is in life. All you have to do is search within yourself to discover the purpose that God created you with.

Sometimes it can seem difficult to identify what your purpose is in life, and that's completely understandable. I mentioned earlier in this chapter that we all have a common purpose in life, which is to bring glory to God. However, our specific, individual purpose can vary from person to person. That's where our uniqueness and individuality comes in. Let me give you a few ways to understand what I mean. Many times, we overlook our purpose. For years, I overlooked my purpose because I was trying to find something that related to an obvious career path. I didn't realize that God had already implanted my purpose in my heart. When I say we overlook our purpose, I am saying that we're looking for something that was never there. Growing up, I was the girl that everyone would come to for advice and want to talk to about life issues. They gravitated to me for some reason, and I always found myself in positions where I had to share a bit of wisdom or insight into their life. Often times, I really did not even have much insight into what they were experiencing; however, it was just something inside of me that drew people to me. At the time, I didn't realize that was a part of my purpose. I struggled for many years pursuing careers that at the end of the day just didn't fulfill me. When I realized what God planted inside of me, I became a life coach and mentor. Nothing else could compare to the joy of helping people understand who they are. What is it that gives you life? What is that thing that makes you come alive? Purpose is the thing that will come naturally to you. It's perfectly interwoven into your passions and your desires. In fact, I believe this is why it's so easy to overlook your purpose because you don't relate it with your passions. It's like the saying goes, "Hidden in plain view."

Before I talk about ways to discover your purpose, I want to identify some factors that indicate that you may not be living your God-given purpose.

1. Do you feel stuck? You want to move forward and change, but it feels like something is holding you back. It's like you fall into a pool of quicksand. You try and reach your hands out to grab hold of the outer rim of the pool but the force of the quicksand is overpowering your reach, and second, by second you sink deeper in until you are completely immersed. You keep grabbing for the outer rim and screaming in hopes someone will hear you and come to your rescue, but no one does. Nothing you do seems to help, and you are unsure of how to move forward. You want it to end but unclear of the "thing" that will turn your situation around. This might be a clear sign that you are not living your purpose.

2. Do you lack joy and fulfillment? Fulfillment generally comes from doing work that is meaningful and rewarding. That can be volunteer work or even a job that allows you to utilize your passion. Of course, there will be certain things we do that won't be as fulfilling, but if your entire life feels incomplete, then you need to look deep within and ask yourself why. If you find yourself going through the motions of life and nothing you do brings

fulfillment, then you have not tapped in your purpose yet. True fulfillment only comes by living your purpose.

3. Are you constantly frustrated? Maybe you feel apathetic about life. You tell yourself things will get better in time. You spend 40 hours or more a week clocking in at work, go home, wake up and do it all over again. You feel like you are aimlessly wandering around trying to find peace or just pull your life together. I know the feeling because I've been there. It doesn't feel good at all. Despite how you feel, just know that you are actually in a great place for God to do a deep work in your life. If you will allow Him by laying all your frustrations, burdens, and cares at His feet, you can begin to discover the life God has for you.

4. Are you living in sin? Sin is by far the greatest issue in your life that will pull you away from walking in God's purpose. It will cause you to feel stuck. It will cause you to lack joy and fulfillment. It will cause you to be constantly frustrated. God did not create you to live in sin; therefore when you are, you will experience a sense of purposelessness. You cannot both, live in sin and walk in God's purpose for your life. There was a time in my life when I was in blatant sin to God. I was a follower of Christ and had gotten entangled with sin because of a series of bad decisions I made. I knew I was wrong but tried to continue serving God anyway. I began to drift away from God or anything that was pertaining to Him. I had no peace at that time. I felt like life was closing in on me and I couldn't breathe. I could not serve God with a clear conscious while being comfortable in my sin. You may be experiencing this and wondering, how do I get out? Until you repent and align your life with God's word, you will always carry that feeling of frustration and lack of fulfillment.

Now, how does one discover his or her purpose? I will share a few ways, but the first thing we must understand is that purpose comes from God and Him alone, the One who created the purpose inside of us. Anything outside of God is just good works and efforts at best. While it's true that we do see a lot of people making an impact in the world doing impressive works, we must also understand that this does not mean that it is necessarily a God-given purpose. You can create a business today that will make you a lot of money, but that does not mean that is your purpose that God has given you, even if you are very successful at it. So let's take a look at a few ways that will help you discover your purpose:

1. Dive into the Word of God. You try to find solutions to your problems without going to the source of who can provide answers. The primary way God speaks to us is through His word. Therefore if you want to know and walk in your purpose you should start with the Bible. I'm not saying that it will tell you to become a doctor or lawyer, but in reading, you will begin to understand God's heart. The Bible helps guide us in walking in our purpose. Psalm 119: 105 reads; "Your word is a lamp to my feet and a light to my path." God's word brings light to your path with each step you take as you journey through life. Essentially, discovering your purpose takes devoted time in reading the word.

2. Prayer. No one wants us to know and walk in our purpose more than God does. After all, He created us with the purpose already inside of us. We just have to be connected to Him to discover it. Begin to seek God in prayer on what your purpose is. You may say, "I have done this countless times, and I'm still confused." Have you been consistent and quiet enough to hear God speak back to you? We often think that prayer is going to God with everything, but we never take time to listen for His direction. Yes, sit down with God, ask questions, and seek wisdom, but make sure you don't get up too soon before He speaks. Remember, He speaks through His word, and He can also speak through people.

3. Identify what you are passionate about. Your passions are generally tied to what God has called you to do. Your purpose involves things you are already good at or come naturally to you. They can be anything, however you're probably struggling with how your passion can be useful. For example, you are passionate

about seeing an end to sex trafficking, therefore, start an organization to end it. God can and will order your steps, but maybe you will need to educate yourself on where to start by doing some research. Ask God for direction on how to turn your passion into useful work for Him.

4. Surround yourself with Kingdom minded people. It's said; God gives you purpose, but people help you discover it and its true. Others on the outside looking in can identify things about you that you may not see. This can be pastors, teacher, leaders, mentors or even peers. Make sure its people you trust and know have your best interest at heart. Nonetheless, it's very hard to discover your purpose when you are alone or isolated. You need people no matter how much you try to deny it. That's why God created others. You were never meant to do life alone.

This is where a lot of people need help and direction. Your purpose is unique and specific to you. This is why the way one goes about accomplishing his or her specific purpose will be totally different from someone else. However, I'm sure you have noticed individuals who have very similar purposes in life. I believe God does this so that His will can be done on earth, just as it is in heaven. The entire world is waiting for you to accomplish something. Yes, the world will miss out on what you have to offer if you fail to rise up and fulfill your purpose. God's desire is for us to live out the purpose He has for us. But make no mistake about it; God's will shall be done. If He has to work through someone else, He will. However, when you make the decision that you will live out your purpose, then not only do you get to reap all the benefits of your obedience, but all the people whose lives you touch get to reap the benefits as well.

What has God called you to accomplish in your lifetime? Don't over-complicate it. Don't over-analyze or overthink it. Just close your eyes, take a deep breath, hold it for about three seconds, and exhale. Whatever that first thing is that comes to your heart of hearts, is probably what God is calling you to. Go ahead and try it right now. Close your eyes and take a deep breath in. What came to your spirit? Write it down. I just wrote down my purpose as well. God has called me to lead ladies who are to be healed and delivered through the power of God. I carry this out through discipleship and hosting in-depth spiritual retreats that aid in women being healed in their heart, so they can be in a fertile place for growth in Christ. Here's why it's important to do this. All along your journey to fulfilling your purpose, you will have opportunities to give up. Not only that, but you will question a lot of things along the way. We all will question the process at some point. Why? Because His thoughts are not our thoughts, nor or His ways our ways. We will all scratch our heads trying to understand why God is taking us down a certain path in life. We will all shed those tears on our pillows trying to make sense of why God would allow certain things to happen to us. Rest assured, all of your experiences and everything you've gone through God will surely use in your life. He's good at using things for His purpose. That's why purpose is all about usefulness. God created you to use you for His glory on earth.

Chapter 3
Roadblocks to Purpose

In this chapter, I am going to cover some of the major roadblocks that we face in life that keep us from living out our purpose. Not only have I encountered these obstacles myself, but many others that I've talked to have also faced these very same roadblocks. These roadblocks have hindered us or slowed us down from fulfilling our purpose in life. We all deal with many roadblocks, but I'll discuss a few of the major ones that I know beyond a shadow of a doubt, you're probably encountering now. I'm going to help set your mind free from those obstacles. If you can get past these roadblocks, you can live a successful life in pursuing and fulfilling the purpose that God has on your life.

The first roadblock and probably one of the most important as I discussed in the previous chapter, is knowing who you are. Knowing who you are is so essential to fulfilling your purpose. Who you are is who you were created to be. A lot of us get stuck at, "Who am I"? Who you are gives way for the purpose that God has placed on your life. Jesus asked his disciples, "Who do you say I am." So my question to you is, who do you say you are and where are you getting your information from? I can go down a list with you, of who I am, but the real question is, do I believe those things to be true of myself. I know that I'm a daughter of the most High King. I'm fearfully and wonderfully made. I am the righteousness of God. I am more than a conqueror through Jesus Christ. I also know that I'm a daughter to my mother. I am a friend to others. I'm a helping hand to those in need and that I am a mentor to women who need guidance. That's who I am, so I'm going to live my life according to who I know God has called me to be so that I can fulfill His purpose for my life. I guarantee if you search the Scriptures and begin to ask God who He created you to be and what your specific purpose is, God's word will unlock those answers in your life. While it is true, God gives us our purpose, the people the people we surround ourselves with can help us discover it. That means ultimately, God is the one who gives you that purpose, but you must be connected to other people who can identify these things inside of you to help draw it out. I mentioned in the previous chapter about discovering purpose. You begin to discover your purpose when you begin to identify those things that come naturally for you, those natural desires and passions that you sometimes overlook. I had someone in my life help identify my passion to see women healed and grow in Christ. Even though that desire was already there I overlooked it. My mind did not automatically connect the two. I believe this is what makes it hard for some people to identify purpose, because they don't have the right people in their lives to help draw it out. Contrary to what the world may say, Jesus is not all that you need. If you did not need people, God would not have created the billions of people on earth for you to have relationships with. God gives purpose and the people that he surrounds us with help us discover it because they can see things that we may not see. It wasn't until I truly got connected to my church and a body of believers and submitted myself to leadership that I really began to see my purpose unfold. You have to first discover it, but then you also have to be equipped with the proper tools that God has given you to be effective at fulfilling your purpose.

Now once you actually discover who you are and what your purpose is, another handful of obstacles comes your way. This is one that every single person reading this book has faced if you're not currently facing it right now in your life. It's the fear of failure. I don't know why the human brain is wired to think that we cannot do something as compared to doing it. It's almost as if our minds are wired for failure. We begin to think, "I can't do this. I can't do this by myself." Millions of questions run through your mind, and they discourage you from moving forward. Fear can be very crippling.

This is something that I dealt with for so many years, and it really held me back from moving forward, and I do not want you to be held back from fulfilling your God-given purpose. There is no time like the present, and there is no time promised to you. You have to get rid of this failure mentality. God never said that you are to do this on your own. If God has called you to something, He will help you do it. It is something that God has placed inside of us and our dependence has to be through Him. Remember God gave you purpose and it is through Him that you will fulfill it. It is impossible to do it on your own and within yourself. When we fail to depend on God and seek guidance to be led by his Holy Spirit, it will seem so overwhelming for us. The word of God says in Philippians 4:13 "I can do all things through Christ who strengthens me." It is by Christ and through Him that you will accomplish your purpose. And trust me I'm a walking testimony that this here is easier said than done; however it is possible.

I dealt with a fear of failure for so long of my life. When I became a believer, and God finally helped me to see what my purpose was, it freaked me out. It freaked me out so bad because I thought this is too much for little old me. No one will listen to me or follow me. "I will fail these people God, how do you expect me to do this?" I did not trust myself nor did I feel properly equipped or trained to do what God had called me to do. My mind constantly told me I could not do this and therefore I believed I couldn't. This leads me to my next few points.

Another roadblock to fulfilling purpose is a poor mindset. The Bible says in Proverbs 23: 7 "As a man thinks in his heart, so is he." I want to stress, what you believe is literally the actions you will portray in your life. Whatever you believe to be true in your mind is the life you will create for yourself, whether it's true or not. But that's the power of your mind. If you can get your mind to believe that you can't do something, then please believe you won't do it even though within you there is the ability to do so. You have already shut yourself off. We are victorious in Christ; however, you will never live a victorious life that God said you could live in Him if your mind continuously believes defeat. If you tell yourself that you're nervous about something, those nervous feelings begin to play out in your life, and then it brings about actions of nervousness because you told yourself that. If we could just get rid of poor thinking, we can accomplish far greater things in our lives. Joyce Myers has a book called *The Battlefield of the Mind*, and I agree that the mind truly is a battlefield. There are so many thoughts roaming and lurking in your mind that you have to combat with every day. Not to sound like I'm coming from a negative standpoint, but I don't believe that we ever get to a place in our lifetime where we don't have to shift our mindsets. I truly believe that it's an everyday pursuit. The Bible says in Luke 9:23 " If anyone desires to come after ME, let him deny himself, and take up his cross daily and follow Me." It's a daily thing, not something we do one time and then think we're good. If we don't set our minds every day, we allow doubt and fear to creep in and hinder us. That is something that every individual in life faces. It doesn't matter who you are. You can be the greatest pastor, preacher, or teacher and you will still deal with the human mind of doubt and fear. With the millions of thoughts that we have every day coming against our purpose, we have to make up in our minds every day to go against those negative thoughts and believe what the word of God says about us. The enemy is fighting against you because He doesn't want to see you live out purpose. As a matter of fact, even with me writing this book, I had to face the mindset of, "Can I really do this?" I speak at different events all the time, but writing a book is much more complex, and when I started I was so excited about it. But then those doubts came in; "Will you really have enough to say, Lisa? Will people really even care enough to read this book and hear what you have to say? Will anyone buy your book? You can't do this Lisa, so why even spend the time and stress yourself out to go ahead and make this happen, when at the end of the day it's just impossible? I had to deal with these thoughts, but I also had to overcome them by constantly telling myself I could do this. I had to keep telling myself this every day I sat down and push past the negativity and doubt. I didn't necessarily have control of those initial thoughts that came into my mind, but I had a choice to believe them or not. Every day you have to tell yourself the truth until the truth drops into your heart and you believe it. It's one thing to know something, it's another thing to actually believe it. You have to tell yourself until you believe it and when you believe it, you have to keep telling yourself because the enemy will continue to bring negative thoughts of doubt to get you to go against what you know and believe to be true.

I remember when I was in school one day and the teacher gave us a pop quiz. Nobody really likes a pop quiz if they have not studied or prepared for it. It just seems to cause so much anxiety and fear if you are unsure if you will pass this test. So I remember in college, my government class teacher called a pop quiz and I did not study for it. I leaned over to the person beside me and said, "I hate pop quizzes. Why don't they tell us?" The person beside me said, "Pop quizzes are only scary if you didn't prepare ahead of time for the test." Now since I wanted this person to agree with me, I grudgingly said, "You're right." But if I had prepared ahead of time, I wouldn't have been in a position to fail. I would've already been prepared with the necessary tools to succeed. Therefore, another major roadblock that we face in fulfilling our purpose is a sense of not being prepared.

Everybody wants to be prepared to do a task that they're being asked to do. If we don't feel that we are prepared or equipped then, of course, we are not going to want to do the task. Even though you may not initially be as prepared as you'd like, you can still take steps to getting there. Just as a baby does not know how to walk, he or she has to take their first step and then their second step and then the third step and so forth until they get the strength and the balance to walk on their own. It is the same way with us. We take one step, we take two steps, and then we get the strength and balance that we need to walk in purpose. This is not done alone. If you want to take steps that will help you prepare for where God is taking you, I say the first place to start is in the house of God. You fulfill your God-given purpose by being connected to your local house, which is your church. Once you are connected to the house of God then you submit to godly leadership who has insight and wisdom. That's why I say mentorship is so important and beneficial.

Get around some godly people that have wisdom and experience that can help identify things in your life as well as equip and train you. You can also take classes or lessons on things that you know God has placed in your heart to do. I wanted to mentor and disciple ladies, so I literally got connected to my church and submitted to my pastors so that they would give direction and insight on what's the best route to go. I began to do research on in-depth spiritual retreats that would cater to the inner healing of ladies because I know that's what God called me to do. Preparation is very crucial to our confidence. Getting submitted to a church, seeking guidance from leadership, and connecting with brothers and sisters in Christ can help you fulfill your God-given purpose. All throughout the Bible they had teachers to show them the way so how much more do we need someone to help us get prepared.

Another huge roadblock or pitfall that we fall into is thinking that we can do it alone. We are better together than we are alone. Since we were never meant to do life alone, it's safe to say we were never meant to do purpose alone, because purpose entails our life. Even though you have a specific purpose here on earth, God still uses others around you to help you fulfill it. Let's look at the greatest example: Jesus. He came to seek and to save those who were lost. He came to die for all mankind. After Jesus died on the cross, His mission was continued through the twelve disciples He raised up. Of course, he went to the Cross alone, because that was something that only He could bear. Yes, God has still called you for a specific purpose, but people help that mission come to pass in your life quicker or more effectively. Jesus dying on the cross was His ultimate purpose, but without His disciples, the gospel message would not have been spread across the world. And we today are still spreading that message. He needed others to help fulfill that purpose. Purpose was never meant to be done alone. You need people!!

As I mentioned before, there are so many roadblocks that we can discuss in this chapter that could probably be a book itself, but there are so many other things that I will touch upon throughout each chapter that will resonate in your heart.

However, the last roadblock I will discuss is inconsistency. Inconsistency will trip you up so quickly. You get on track, but then life happens, and you get off track and then it becomes a cycle of inconsistency. It creates in us an unenthusiastic spirit about moving forward. Inconsistency gives room for complacency and laziness. You have to be consistent in pursuing and proactive in going after your purpose. You have to stay the course, or it will be too easy for detours to come in your life and distract you.

So how do you stay consistent? You have to create specific and realistic goals that can be measured. What I mean by measured is that you have to be able to determine if you met the goal or not. Next, you want to set a schedule for how you're going to reach these goals. Be intentional about sending reminders to help you stay on track. We all have busy lives nowadays, so it is best to set reminders to help you stay on track. Do not overcommit. Only take on what is within your allowed time frame. You have to be in control of your time or your time will control you. You have to know what to say no to. If you set your mind to do something between a certain timeframe be sure to stick with it. We know that life emergencies and situations happen that you cannot control and that's understandable, but for the most part, you can control certain things, and you shouldn't allow anything to interrupt your schedule unless you absolutely have to.

Chapter 4
Know Yourself

Have you ever found yourself in an elevator or at an event or any place where you would come into contact with a stranger, and the opportunity to meet someone new presents itself? I've always found it a bit awkward to spark a good conversation with others in those moments. However, I often times manage to say something. Tell me if you can relate to this experience:

John: Hello, how are you?

Kim: I'm fine, thank you.

Kim: My name is Kim and you?

John: It's John. Nice to meet you.

Kim: Same to you.

John: So, what is it that you do?

Isn't it funny how when we meet someone for the first time, one of the main questions we ask is, "What is it that you do"? We typically tell them what we do, and assumptions are made of who you are based on your career or job. People are generally impressed by your title or position: the fancier, the better, so you seek to obtain higher positions because it supposedly gives you more significance or holds you in a more honorable regard. As a society, we have become more concerned with what a person does than who they really are. You have been programmed to place more importance on what a person does than getting to know the core of a person's true self. In fact, if you were to ask a person "Who are you?" they would probably be offended or confused and unable to answer the question. However, they can give you in full detail as to what they do.

It's important to realize that who you are is far more important than what you do. Who you are will always direct what you are to do, but what you do may not always reflect your true self. Though there are many aspects of who a person is, we have to be able to define the core of who we are. To truly answer this question, you have to know yourself and be able to convey it in a way that you feel best defines you. There is a man in the bible named John, commonly referred to as John the Baptist. He was mistaken for being the Messiah, which means the Christ. Each time he was asked if he was the Messiah, he would say no, "I am not the Messiah." They aggressively asked, "Then who are you?" He explained that he was a voice shouting in the wilderness; clearing the way for the Lord's coming. John did not take on the identity of someone else because he knew exactly who he was.

We take on the identity of others because we don't really know who we are. That's because your identity lies in Christ. There is no way to identify yourself outside of your Creator; the One who made you and knows you best. Our personal experiences in life more than often shape how we see our identity and ourselves. The problem with this is that past mistakes and experiences are not definitive. My pastor once said this statement, and it reigns true, "Failure is an event, not a person." It's so hard to transition our mind from lies to truth when that is all we have believed for so long. Listed below are lies that we have believed and caused us to doubt who we are:

- You are a failure
- You are not enough
- You are worthless
- You are not loved
- Nobody wants you
- You will always be alone
- Your life will never amount to any importance

We've all heard, "sticks and stones may break my bones, but words will never hurt me." That is the biggest lie of them all because words sink deep into our hearts and last even after scars have healed. It shapes our reality of who we are instead of allowing the word of God to shape us. Who does the word of God say you are?

- "For a righteous man falls seven times and rises again, But the wicked stumble in time of calamity." Proverbs 24:16
- "I will praise thee, for I am fearfully and wonderfully made: marvelous are thy works, And my soul knoweth right well." Psalm 139:14
- "So don't be afraid, you are more valuable to God than a whole flock of sparrows." Matthew 10:31
- "The Lord appeared to us in the past, saying: I have loved you with an everlasting love: I have drawn you with unfailing kindness" Jeremiah 31:3
- "God paid a high price for you, so don't be enslaved by the world." 1 Corinthians 7:23
- Be strong and courageous. Do not be afraid or terrified because of them, for the Lord your God goes with you; he will never leave you nor forsake you." Deuteronomy 31:6
- "I, the Lord have called you for a righteous purpose, and I will take hold of your hand. I will keep you and appoint you to be a covenant for the people and a light to the nations." Isaiah 42:6

The word of God is full of declarations for your life. The only way to know what He says about you is to read His word.

There was a time in my life when I had no utter idea who I was. I was lost and confused, and no one could really help me. I was shy. I was lost. I was afraid to speak. I had low self-esteem. I didn't think I was pretty. When you are not walking in who God created you to be, you are living a false reality of who you are, and that's the life you create for yourself. I said I walked about shy and afraid to speak. The enemy loved nothing more than to keep my mouth trapped so I wouldn't speak he truth of God's word. I was called to speak to multitudes of people, but there was literally no way I could do that when I was shy and afraid to speak.

Even after you have knowledge of who God says you are, it still has to resonate in your heart until you believe it. God can deliver you, but you can still get entangled with the lies of the enemy later in life if you are not careful. The enemy will whisper in your ear, "Remember that time when your parents weren't there for you. Remember that time when no one wanted you." And if you aren't careful, you will buy into his lies every time. People buy into the lies every day even after God has set them free.

Why is it so important to know who you are? Your identity has everything to do with your purpose. In order to do what you were created to do, you have to know who you are. You will act according to who you believe you are. God is waiting for us to become who He created us to be so we can impact the lives we were meant to see changed.

Chapter 5
Identify Your Strengths

It was the summer of 2011; I was at my church in Louisiana when I was asked to meet with my pastor's wife about working on their team for an internship. It was a leadership/discipleship program. I was asked to be on the team that would be responsible for overseeing a home that would house a group of young ladies that would be participating in the internship. In our first meeting, the pastor's wife asked us about our strengths and weaknesses. The pastor then asked us to take a test to identify our strengths. It was explained to me that any great leader should be able to identify their strengths because that's the area that you will be most effective. "We never want to place you in the area that you're going to be ineffective because it does you no justice nor the ones around you," the pastor went on to explain.

So, I went home that day, and I took the test. The results that I received made complete sense and bore witness to who I was. It described me right on. Prior to taking that test, I may have had an inclination of my strengths, but now I was able to see it in a clearer way. My strengths became more identifiable for me, and I was now able to put them in words.

My strengths were things that came naturally to me because it was a part of who I was. I didn't have to try and work on possessing these things because it was the core of who I was. Likewise, your strengths are things about you that you are naturally good at or positions that you naturally operate in. To further explain, I'll share a few of my strengths with you that I discovered through the test I took. I am naturally good at relating to others. I love building close relationships with people that I can relate to or they relate to me. I also have a strong belief system, which means that I have a set of core values that are unwavering or unchanging regardless of who I come in contact with. Those core values, to me, define a greater purpose because they come from a greater source, which is my God. I'm also a developer. I identify the potential in others, and I love to cultivate that potential. The heart of my church was to build leaders. That's why we even had the internship I mentioned above. While in the internship, a friend of mine asked me, "How do you build leaders so effectively?" I wasn't able to eloquently put it in words at the time, so I simply said, "I don't know; it just comes naturally for me." However, for her, it didn't come as naturally because we didn't share the same strength. She had a different set of strengths that I didn't identify with. It didn't make either of us better or worse than the other, it was just being able to identify where her strengths were so that she could be more effective in that capacity. I believe that one of the things that made me so effective in building leaders was my understanding that building leaders is all about relating, developing others, cultivating trust, and building with them. For me, those things were the core of who I was.

On the flipside, I was not strong in the area of planning events or even having a creative eye for decorating. At times I would feel like something was wrong with me because certain people were extremely good at it, while I seemed to crumble under the weight of it. That may not seem like a big deal to you, but in the internship program that I mentioned, a portion of what we did consisted of us planning for events. You can imagine how I felt when I would be tasked with yet another event. I would stand there with this clueless look in my eyes, hoping that no one else could notice it. I found the task to be quite intimidating, mostly because I knew that my execution of the task would reveal an area of weakness for me. Planning for an event or decorating at an event was definitely not something that came naturally to me. Therefore, it was not one of my strengths. Your strengths will be those things that come naturally to you, and they are already a part of who you are. This is a statement that I have come to live by: "The best way to see a person flourish is to allow them to grow or operate in their strengths."

We need to understand that sometimes our strengths can also be a weakness. I know that may sound a bit confusing, but I'll explain. A person who's a great analytical thinker can sometimes overthink situations. A person who is very decisive can sometimes neglect the perspectives of others. In these two examples, you can see where a person's strengths can also become their weaknesses if they are not careful. Why is that? If we don't yield our strengths to the Lord, they become imbalanced. We must surrender our strengths and our entire beings to the Lord in order for everything to remain in the right perspective.

I believe to identify your strengths better; you must start with a common strength that we should all possess. This strength is a cornerstone in your life, and without it, it can be hard for you to identify any other strength that you possess accurately. The common strength that I'm talking about is the joy that comes from within. For the remainder of this chapter, I want to share with you about the joy of the Lord, and more importantly, about the strength that we have when we truly possess His joy.

Nehemiah 8:10 reads, "Do not sorrow for the joy of the Lord is your strength." I will reckon with you that the source of any strength that you will have in life stems from joy. Joy comes from the depths of your soul, knowing that there is a God in heaven that is with you and on your side and fighting for you. It's important to note here that joy should never be confused with happiness. Happiness is only a temporary emotion, based off of our current circumstances. Joy is everlasting and is unconditional because it is a state of being. Your joy is not determined by your feelings or your circumstances. That's why you can have joy in the midst of your deepest struggles because you know that God is with you; the joy that comes with knowing that God is with you and gives you the strength to keep going. You can see people going through hell but still find the strength to pick themselves up and move forward. That's because joy is not dependent on your current situation but is the very source of your strength.

Chapter 6
Identify Your Weaknesses

"And He said to me, "My grace is sufficient for you, for My strength is made perfect in weakness." Therefore most gladly I will rather boast in my infirmities, that the power of Christ may rest upon me. Therefore I take pleasure in infirmities, in reproaches, in needs, in persecutions, in distresses, for Christ's sake. For when I am weak, then I am strong." 2 Corinthians 12:9-10

We often tend to view weakness as a bad thing because no one likes to display any signs of weakness in themselves. However, the truth is that we all have weaknesses; just the same as we all have strengths. Therefore, displaying our weaknesses cannot be so much of a bad thing as it is understanding them.

In the above scripture, Paul says that he will gladly boast in his weaknesses. Our weaknesses give room for Christ's power to work through us on His behalf. But what are the weaknesses that Paul describes? Allow me to clarify exactly what those are. Paul is not talking about weaknesses in the sense of sin. He's not saying that Christ will make you strong so you can endure through your sin. It's not talking about sin, ungodly behavior or choices. Rather, Paul is talking about situations in our lives that have the potential to make us look weak as Christians. In this passage, what Paul is talking about are the circumstances or experiences that we face in life that we would change if we had it in our power to do so. In other words, he's referring to the calamities and hardships that we encounter in life as believers. However, we can also be weak in the areas of sin. The things that we struggle with internally that causes us to fall into sin.

We can also be weak in the area of abilities. I was at my church, and we were planning for a huge conference. We needed all hands on deck. Since I was a part of the leadership team, that meant my hands needed to be on deck as well. They needed decorating ideas for the conference, which meant they needed us to be creative. The second I heard them mention where the need was I could have stuck my head in the ground like an ostrich. I do not have an ounce of creativity when it comes to decorating. My mind draws a blank, and I cannot tell you whether something looks good or not. All color coordination flies out the window, and I'm at a loss for ideas that someone would actually appreciate. One of my least favorite questions, when I'm in these types of situations, is, "Lisa, what do you think about this?" I literally cannot comprehend the concept of decorating for anything. I know that probably sounds bad, but it's true.

I wondered if people began to think there was something wrong with me. I had been that way my entire life. Some people have an eye for that, and there are some people, like me, who don't have a clue what's going on. Nonetheless, I recognized this as one of my weak areas. Some people are just so good at decorating; it blows me away at how effortless they make it appear. I have no idea how they can do it. But just as a person may be weak in one area, they are strong in other areas. It is okay to have weaknesses. It doesn't mean that anything is wrong with a person. Everyone has weak areas, and I had to find that out along the way. I also learned that those things that I'm good at, someone else might have a hard time comprehending how I am able to do those things.

When I was ready to write this book, I knew that writing was not a strong area of mine. I knew I would need some help. It wasn't so much that I was a bad writer, it was more so a matter of how long it would take me to formulate my thoughts and ideas and get them down on paper and have it all make sense to the reader. It wasn't easy, but I knew that it was something I would have to do. In fact, I would say that it was something that I needed to do. Here's why.

Much like you, I have weaknesses too; we all do. The dilemma is not in having weaknesses. The dilemma is in what are we doing about our weaknesses. My goal in this chapter is to help you strengthen those areas where you are weak. I heard Les Brown once say, "You can always better your best." If you can learn how to strengthen your weaknesses, then you will also learn how to strengthen your strengths. I know that sounds strange, but it's so true! You are not stuck with your weaknesses. Your weaknesses do not have to remain your weaknesses for the rest of your life. You can do something about them. Here's how.

First, be honest with yourself. Don't live in denial about your weaknesses. There's almost nothing more annoying than being around someone who is completely oblivious to his or her weaknesses. Have you ever been in that situation? Have you ever been with someone who has a poor sense of direction, yet they will never admit it? They always want to drive, but you know they will get lost. Everyone knows it. But if you try to point it out, they get offended and start blaming Google Maps and the GPS and everything else under the sun.

You have to be humble enough to get honest and recognize those areas in your life that need strengthening. Perhaps it's in your time management? Perhaps it's in the way you treat others? Perhaps it's in your self-discipline? Perhaps it's in your ability to put others above yourself? I don't know what your specific area of weakness is; all I know is that you have weaknesses in your life that you first have to honestly identify if you're ever going to strengthen them.

Second, you will need to do what I did when I started writing this book. I found some help. Get with some other people who are strong in the areas where you are weak. If reading is your weakness, find someone who reads well. If making friends is your weakness, find someone who has plenty of friends. If writing is your weakness, find someone who writes well. Whatever your weakness is, I can guarantee you that there's someone in your life who excels in that area. It's how God designed your life, He knew what you would need before you knew you would need it.

Third, you need to resolve within yourself not to remain the same. Determine that no matter what, this will not be a weakness of yours forever. I'm not suggesting that you will become a master in every area where you are weak. I'm simply saying that it won't be a weakness of yours anymore. If we were to put it in terms of a scale between one and ten, where weakness is anything that scores a three or below, you want to move those areas from a score of three to a score of five or six.

Fourth, you will want to continue to work on that weakness. The only way you build muscle is by doing the correct exercises, consistently. Determining not to allow this to remain a weakness of yours is not enough. You must do something about it. For me, writing was a weakness; therefore, I had to keep writing. I had to exercise that weak muscle, it was the only way I could strengthen it. I couldn't write just one paragraph in my book and expect that weakness to become a strength of mine. I had to write over twenty thousand words, and the best part about it is that I'm still writing so that I can strengthen that area even more.

The fifth and final thing you will need to do is change your language. The longer you continue to tell yourself that you are weak in this area, the longer you will remain weak in that area. Change your belief, change your language, and change your results. Try this instead, "This is an area that I'm getting stronger in. I'm not exactly where I want to be right now, but in the next month, I will be much stronger in this area." If I was ever going to finish writing this book, I had to change my belief about my own ability to write. The more I would tell myself that I was going to write this book and that I could do it, the more I started to believe it. I would constantly speak positive words over myself as I wrote this book to reassure and encourage myself that I was becoming a better writer and that I could accomplish this goal until I did. And because I put these five simple steps into practice in my own life, I now have to privilege of sharing with you how to strengthen your weaknesses as well.

Chapter 7
Humility of Purpose

Sadly, this is where a lot of people make their downfall from grace and hinder themselves from fulfilling their purpose in life. We can all potentially get puffed up with pride, to the point where we think we can accomplish God's purpose for our lives without Him. Humility is a vital part of knowing who you are and walking in your purpose. Without humility, we are not operating from the right spirit or heart, and that will keep God from using us in the way He always intended. If you want to be used by God then walking in humility is the most crucial virtue you can possess.

Humility is an inward grace of the soul that allows one to think of himself no more highly than he ought to think. Romans 12:3 says "Do not think of yourself more highly than you ought, but rather think of yourself with sober judgment." This is not saying we can't think highly of ourselves; rather, it's instructing us to think in the right estimation of ourselves.

A humble heart is wholly surrendered to and dependent on God because we realize just how much we need Him. Many times you will be tempted to depend on your own abilities, accomplishments, and knowledge instead of depending on God. When you depend on these things, it creates a false image in your mind of who you are. You are NOT your accomplishments or abilities, you are to be the reflection of Christ.

When you measure yourself according to the word of God, you see just how much you need Him. I find there are far too many people in the world who are addicted to glorifying themselves or being glorified by others. I'm sure you know someone who loves to talk about themselves more than any other topic. In this chapter, I want to discuss a few reasons why people get caught up in pride and then what it means to walk in humility.

One of the reasons people get puffed up with pride or think they should be glorified is because of knowledge. They say knowledge is power and that is only partially true. The more you know, the more you can accomplish, but knowledge must never be confused with FAITH. A person can be very knowledgeable but immature at the same time. You can know everything there is to know about a subject and know very little about the Lord and your own need for grace. When knowledgeable people look at themselves, they're tempted to see someone that rarely needs help, but God's Word reveals that we have a deceitful and desperately sick heart that needs daily rescue. (Jeremiah 17:9). We see Paul in Philippians 3:4-11, turns his back on knowledge and his status position because he knew that knowing Christ was far greater.

Praise God if He has gifted you with a powerful brain! However, continue to pursue the knowledge for His glory and for the good of others. Do not think of yourself more highly than you ought.

The second reason people often find themselves operating in pride is because of experiences. The more you experience, the more confidence you develop. You're less and less intimidated by life because you've seen more, but there's a huge difference between wisdom gained from experience and spiritual wisdom gained from Christ. What I mean by this is that just because you've been through some things in life doesn't mean you've dealt with it, or will deal with it, in a God-honoring way. God's Word reveals that we're all still spiritually immature in some capacity and will never stop learning and growing until Jesus returns (Philippians 1:6). I have experienced a lot in my short time on earth, but I'm still open to learning from people that have walked this walk a little longer than me.

The third reason people get puffed up with pride is because of success. Being successful is something I believe you should pursue. I know it's a wonderful blessing when you achieve success, but it can also be a dangerous thing. Some successful people are rarely humble because they take credit for what only God can produce. The Bible never equates success, in life or ministry, with personal holiness. Therefore, it's very possible for you to be very successful and very distant from God at the same time, even as a professing Christian.

When successful people at themselves, they're tempted to see someone who deserves all that they've earned, but God's Word reveals that every good gift comes from the Father (James 1:17), and none of us actually want what we truly deserve (Psalm 103:10). We should dream big, make money, and impact lots of people's lives, but remember that you didn't get it on your own.

The fourth thing I see that causes people to get puffed up is recognition. The praise and recognition of others is music to our ears because we selfishly love to be glorified and can be kept awake at night by the negative opinions others have of us. As a result, we often make choices that are driven by the approval of men rather than the approval of God (John 12:43).

When popular people look at themselves, they're tempted to see someone who has "arrived" because people treat them as if they're someone more important or significant than others. But God's Word reveals that we all have fallen short of the only standard that matters (Romans 3:23). It's not an evil thing to be spoken highly of. Christians should strive to be respected in and out of the church, but even if others recognize you, don't think of yourself more highly than you ought.

Philippians 2:1-8 says, "Therefore if you have any encouragement from being united with Christ, if any comfort from his love, if any common sharing in the Spirit, if any tenderness and compassion, then make my joy complete by being like-minded, having the same love, being one in spirit and of one mind. Do nothing out of selfish ambition or vain conceit. Rather, in humility value others above yourselves, not looking to your own interests but each of you to the interests of the others. In your relationships with one another, have the same mindset as Christ Jesus: Who, being in very nature of God, did not consider equality with God something to be used to his own advantage; rather, he made himself nothing by taking the very nature of a servant, being made in human likeness. And being found in appearance as a man, he humbled himself by becoming obedient to death—even death on a cross!"

There is no greater example of humility than what we see in the life of Christ and read here in this above passage. This is the heart you must truly want and possess if you want God to use you.

How do we walk in humility?

Have a heart change.

You should always ask yourself, "What needs to change in my heart?" Humility recognizes that there is a change that needs to be made. Humility is a matter of the heart and cannot be displayed unless it's transformed. It's the heart that God begins with. What needs to change or be healed in your heart so you can allow the characteristics of God to flow in and through you?

Value others.

Value others above yourself as Christ did. Don't look out only for your interest, but look out for the interests of others. Don't think you are better than anyone because you hold a certain position or status. Jesus, who was God, did not equate Himself as God but considered Himself nothing, taking on the nature of a servant when He, in fact, had every right to take on the nature of King. We don't have that right. We should never look down on anyone because we all are mere flesh, made from dust.

Serve others.

When you serve others, you take your mind off of self. You become more aware that you are not the center of the universe. Serving postures you to lift up others, which is exactly what Jesus did. Even though He had reason to be served, He set an example for us by saying He came to serve and not be served. Too often we think we need to be served when Jesus Himself didn't even come to be served. Servanthood is a true sign of humility.

Walk in obedience.

There is no greater way to walk in humility than to be obedient. Jesus humbled Himself in obedience to the point of death on the cross. His willingness to surrender to a greater plan than what He might have thought was best is a wonderful example for us to follow as Christians. The cross of Christ was painful and gruesome, but He knew it was worth it. Sometimes God, or even people, will tell us things that will be painful to our flesh nature or desires, but we have to surrender and be obedient. No one likes having to deal with a disobedient child. Their behavior makes you want to say, "The audacity of you! Don't you know I have your best interest at heart?" When we are obedient, even to things that we don't fully understand or appreciate at the moment, it shows we are willing to allow ourselves to be led to a greater purpose.

Humility is kind-hearted, gentle, loving, and forgiving. Pride, however, exalts itself above others, which is rooted in insecurity and causes us to depend on characteristics that have nothing to do with the heart of God.

I can understand why it's easier to run to these insecurities instead of the Word of God. It gives you a false view of your character and sense of approval, while the word of God exposes your weaknesses, flaws, and failures so that you can see the power of God and your need for Him in every area of your life. It is the Cross of Christ that frees you from fear of your insecurities and weaknesses being exposed. Christ has the power to heal you so that your heart can be transformed into the likeness of Christ and you can begin to walk in humility to accomplish His purpose for your life.

Section Two:

DEVELOP

Chapter 8
Mindset

We hear all the time how huge of an impact our thought life has on us, and it's true. Our thoughts control our entire life. It goes so far beyond just having a negative thought. I want to help you see where these thoughts stem from, how they shape your life, and how powerful the mind is. I remember I was in my sophomore year of college; some of the best times of your life, right? I have always been an honor roll student all throughout school, so it was common for me in college as well. I had given my life to the Lord in my first semester of college. I was going to church, serving, meeting people and making friendships. Everything was going pretty good, to say the least. I was in a relationship with a guy who I would've married if it had not been for the Lord telling me to cut it off. We had cell phone plans together and everything. Between the end of my freshman year and the beginning of my sophomore year, I'd gone home for the summer and I think this is where everything started to transpire in my mind. Before I left campus, I heard a message on relationships, and it caused me to make a decision to break things off with the guy I was currently dating. In doing that I wanted to cancel our cell phone plans together. I went home and wrote a check to him to cancel the line that he had for me. I felt good about the decision I made, but after about a week or so of not hearing from him, I thought maybe he didn't really care about me. Why wouldn't he call to check up on me? That little incident opened up a floodgate of thoughts and emotions that were triggered from my past. Feelings of being unwanted, unloved and rejected even though I was the one who cut it off. I began to think that no one cared about me so why should I care about myself? Shortly after I returned back to school, I was no longer enthusiastic, and I felt very indifferent. I registered for my classes and thought some would be very challenging, and I didn't necessarily want to deal with it, so I made up in my mind that these classes would be too hard so why even bother. "After all no one cares if I do well or not." I had four classes that semester, and I failed every one. I went into that semester thinking no one cared about me, and that I couldn't do it anyway so why bother. Those thoughts shaped every decision that I made even though I had the potential to once again, do very well. I allowed myself to be limited, and therefore my potential was limited.

I want to dig into the mind really quick and give you a few definitions. The mind is talked about a lot, but I don't know if we've ever really taken the time to look up the definition of mindset or mind or anything of that matter. The medical definition of the mind says that it is the element in an individual that feels, perceives, thinks, wills, and especially reasons. The mind is defined as the element of a person that enables them to be aware of the world and their experiences, to think, and to feel: the faculty of consciousness and thought life. The mindset is defined as an established set of attitudes held by someone. Now I want to focus in on this word "established" as it refers to the mindset. If something has been established that means it is rooted and didn't happen overnight. Something that is established takes time; it has been built upon and set in over time. We, as adults, have certain mindsets that have been established over our lifetime. You have thoughts that are hidden in your subconscious mind that are dictating your reality and your behavior.

Whatever belief you hold in your mind will become your reality. Your subconscious mind cannot really tell whether an event is actually true or not. That's right, your mind cannot tell whether an actual event is happening or if you are just thinking about it, but your body reacts to it nevertheless. We were all kids at once, and I'm sure you can remember the Freddy Krueger movies. Freddy Krueger would only attack people in their sleep. They would try so hard not to fall asleep because they knew Freddy was coming. Why wouldn't he attack them while they were awake? It wasn't until I was older that I realized that he could only attack in dreams because none of it was real. It was all in their subconscious mind. They became fearful, they would sweat, their heart would race, but they weren't in any real danger at all. Some of the people in those dreams would get physically injured and even die. However, this event was only taking place in their mind, but their mind didn't know that. Therefore their bodies reacted as though it was real. Once they would awake, it was all over. He was not able to attack them while they were awake. All physical reality is made up of energy. Your thoughts are energy and have the greatest influence on your behavior in life. Their subconscious minds literally caused them to think that a situation was real even though it wasn't and their body physically reacted to it to the point of bodily harm. That's how powerful your mind is and has an effect on your life. If you think fear, your body will give off that energy and shape your actions to become fearful to the point that you can actually put yourself in a harmful situation that you may have never been in.

Whatever belief you hold in your mind will become your reality. Since your mind shapes how you behave let's talk about what shapes your mind. Everything that you have been exposed to your entire life, from what you see, to what you feel, to what you hear, to what you taste, to what you touch all shapes your mind. Most of your lives the media have planted messages in your mind whether good or bad. From childhood, you've seen images of murder, sex, drugs, and profanity, which infiltrates your subconscious mind. When I was a child, I would watch a lot of horror movies, which planted fear in my mind. Whenever the lights were off, or I heard something I would automatically be scared because my subconscious mind created a feeling that something was not right. I believe that's why we have a lot of kids who are afraid of the dark even though there's no real harm. I am not necessarily saying that we are going to go out and commit murder if we see it on TV, but if all we see are hostile situations of anger, and murder it subconsciously creates a hostile mentality to the way we react to things and the way we respond to them.

So back to the gentleman in the beginning that I had broke things off with. I had made a conscious decision not to listen to any music that would stimulate any thoughts of that previous relationship. One of my friends at the time called me up and told me about this new song I just had to listen to. She promised me it was not bad. I said no it's okay I don't really want to listen to it, but she insisted that it was okay. I said I would go ahead and listen to it. I put the song on, and I'm not really sure the name of it, but it was talking about how you had it bad for a person in the relationship. By the end of the song, I wanted to call him to apologize and make things right to continue that relationship that I knew the Lord had told me to cut off. What happened with that song is it planted thoughts in my mind that caused a reaction in my behavior. A lot of the things you listen to create the same type of behavior in your life because what you are hearing is shaping your mind and thoughts. The same can be said for anxiety. I do not believe that any situation is the cause of anxiety; I believe it's the psychological reaction to the situation that causes anxiety. If your mind is calm in the midst of the situation it will not cause a hostile reaction however if your mind is filled with fear then it will create anxiety reactions. Two people can endure the same event but have different reactions because of how your mind is programmed. Now, this can go both ways, our thoughts can be impacted positively as well. On average we have about 60,000 thoughts a day. That is a lot. About how many of those thoughts do you believe are positive? Maybe a few if we had to count on hand. Our mind is constantly thinking and pulling from established sets of attitudes that have occurred over the duration of our lifetime. The goal is to truly understand how our mindset shapes how we behave. The Bible does say in Proverbs 23:7 "For as he thinks in his heart, so is he." As you think you are, so you shall be. Your thoughts have the power to shape your life positively or negatively. With the thousands of thoughts we have each day it is important that you make sure what you are being exposed to or what you are allowing to shape your mind creates godly, positive, encouraging, uplifting thoughts so that's the type of life you will live.

    If you want to live a victorious, fearless life the way you were created to, then you must set your mind every day on those things that will positively shape your life. Remember you have an established set of attitudes that are stemmed from as early as childhood shaping your mind today and not always in a positive way. Your mind has to be renewed and transformed, and that only comes by renewing your mind with the word of God. This is not a one time "I can do it" mentality. For every one positive thought you have, there are hundreds, possibly even thousands, of negative thoughts combating to get you to fail in life. Everything that you have been exposed to that has shaped your mind literally has to be renewed with a right perspective. The only way to get rid of a poor mindset is to allow the truth of God's word to resonate in your heart and transform your mind. The more truth you allow to shape your mind the more it pushes out the negativity so that you can live the life that God has called you to live. The Bible says in 2 Corinthians 10:5 "We demolish arguments and every pretension that sets itself up against the knowledge of God, and we take captive every thought to make it obedient to Christ." This means you have to take control of your thoughts and submit them to the truth of what Christ has to say. The way you live, and your behavior, will not change unless your mind changes first.

Chapter 9
Core Habits

Your core habits are very vital when it comes to you fulfilling your purpose and living the life God intended you to live here on earth. It is important that you establish a set of core habits that will work best for you. These habits are what will get you to where you need to go. Your core habits may be slightly different from someone else's, but there are a few things that should be core for everyone who is trying to fulfill their purpose in life. Your core habits are your regular tendencies or practices in life that can actually make or break your spiritual and/or personal life.

One of the most practical and simple habits that we should develop, but yet can seem so hard to do, is getting proper rest. Rest is so important to the functionality of an individual. Without proper rest, it throws everything off. If you're sluggish and tired and can't function correctly, you are not able to work to your best ability. I say this is one of the hardest because not many people get even six hours of sleep a night. So they're constantly tired and can't focus as well as they should. One of the key factors in getting proper rest for the night is starting early. In fact, I would even encourage you to start the night before. Preparation is key to getting a good night's rest. Setting your clothes out at night will help you in the morning because you'll already have your outfit set for the day. Likewise, packing your lunch the night before saves time in the morning because you're not standing in front of the refrigerator trying to figure out what you will eat that day. Shutting down all media and social outlets by no later than 9 o'clock is a great way to make sure you're getting to bed at a reasonable time. I know that we constantly want to check social media all throughout the day and night, but it really affects our ability to be able to shut down and go to sleep. If you work a full-time job, you probably have to be there between seven and eight in the morning. Therefore, a good time to be in bed would probably be anywhere between nine and ten the night before. Getting a full eight hours is best for the body; however, we're doing pretty well if we can get at least six to seven hours. Getting a good night's rest tonight really helps set the tone for your tomorrow. You want to be energized, fully alert, and ready to take on the day.

The next habit you should establish is being consistent in the Word of God and prayer. It goes without saying that this is extremely important in your life. This affects your spiritual life, which in turn, greatly impacts your physical life. The best way to accomplish your God-given purpose is through Him. Getting to know Him and allowing Him to deposit into your life continually. The only way to truly stay connected to what God is doing and speaking is to be consistent in His word and prayer. That's why getting the proper rest is so important because we want to be able to get up and spend time with the Lord daily. When we're tired, we are generally prone to snooze for an extra five minutes, and another five minutes, and then before you know it, were running late and we ultimately miss that time with the Lord. You've hit snooze one too many times, and now you've started your day without the most important thing that could revive your soul. Even if it is only five to ten minutes in the morning of reading the word, that's better than nothing. I tell people all the time, you don't have to spend hours and hours in prayer, but you should spend some time with the Lord each day.

Next, you should always start with the end goal in mind. When you have your end goal, it helps you to be able to plan better and set smaller goals along the way to help you meet your end goal. To some, it may actually sound backwards to start with the end before the beginning, but it helps you to begin each day with a clear vision and direction of your destination. One way to do this is to develop a mission statement for your life. It helps you to refocus, set up attainable goals and set a clear path in the direction of where you want to go. Once you have your first mission statement written down, you have to actually act upon it.

Take initiative and move. Once you have everything laid out, then you have to actually act upon it. This is where a lot of people get stuck, because they don't act. The only way to do something that you have never done before is to simply do it. So many times, we get caught up on not knowing the first thing about doing something, and we hinder ourselves by thinking that we need to wait until we get all the information and then move. Act, and you will learn along the way. But if you wait until you have everything right, chances are you will never move, and you will be sitting on your vision or your purpose for years to come. You have to set a personal habit in your life of taking initiative and moving. God gives us a vision, and He may even help us with the steps, but He does not make us do it. We have to do that on our own. There has to be urgency or an understanding of how important this is for you.

Make it a habit of encouraging yourself. We have to make a habit of telling ourselves that we can do this, not to give up, and to keep on pushing. I talk to myself all the time because there are so many moments where I want to give up, where I don't see how this is going to come to pass, but then I begin to tell myself, "You can do this, Lisa." Self-talk is actually good for the soul as long as it's positive self-talk. We get enough negative talk from others. There's no need for us to do it also. So make it a habit of encouraging yourself daily.

Develop the habit of being kind to everyone. This is not a common habit that we think about when we talk about establishing habits that will help you be successful. We generally think about things that will set us up personally for success, which is definitely true. However, we have to remember that everything we do will involve people. From the people that are ahead of us, or the people that we will work with on our teams and peers, to the people that we are reaching out to in hopes of making an impact. Everything we do involves people, and therefore it is essential to make a habit of being kind to everyone. You may say to yourself, "I'm not a people's person," and that's fine, but be a person that's about people. Whether you are in the forefront surrounded by people on a day-to-day basis or whether you're behind the desk not surrounded by as many, trust that you will still interact with people. So all I'm saying is, regardless of how many people you interact with each day, be kind to those people because we never know who we'll need or who will need us.

Chapter 10
Walking in Integrity

Integrity is probably one of the most important chapters in this entire book. Why? It's not something that we really hear much about anymore. Very few people really understand what it means to walk in integrity. Your gifts and your calling will never take you further than where your integrity can keep you. I've seen a lot of great men and women fall or forfeit the purpose of God on their lives because they failed to walk in integrity.

We live in a world where compromise is on the rise and integrity is a lost art. It's quite sad when I think about the few people I know who actually walk in integrity. How many people do you know who truly walk in integrity? It's probably not many. Our nature desires to compromise, sin, and cut corners. We put ourselves in situations that cause us to compromise instead of standing strong in our convictions. The problem with that is, few people really have any type of convictions anymore.

In this chapter, I want to talk to you about character, conviction, compromise, and integrity and how they all work together.

Character is moral quality; having standards of behavior or beliefs concerning what is right or wrong and acceptable versus not acceptable. Rest assured, every person has what we call character, it's just a matter of whether they have good character or not. When we think about a person who has good character, one quality that we would likely all agree on is honesty. We've all heard it said, "Honesty is the best policy," and this is correct. I would like to take it a step further and say that honesty is a requirement for any great leader. A dishonest person can never be trusted. If you are not a person of honesty, God won't be able to trust you with His purpose on your life because His calling always pertains to people. If people can't trust you they will never want to work alongside you or follow you. No one wants to be around a dishonest person. Being honest is not just being honest to the people that you feel can offer you something; you must be honest and fair with all people, even the ones that cannot do anything for you. That shows true character. Sometimes people believe that being dishonest, even if it's just a little here and there, will help them reach the top of their organization or industry. But if, in being dishonest you get to the top, you will always know that you don't really belong there, and there is no joy or satisfaction in knowing that you falsified your way to a place that if you had been truthful, you might have never been. You must choose to be honest about who you really are.

Loyalty is another quality that speaks volumes of a person with good character. We all know how common it is for others to let us down. Loyalty says I'll stick with you no matter what comes our way. I will be committed to you to the end.

Consistency is another great characteristic. We all love a person who is consistent and not fickle; changing every time the sun rises. People like that are hard to relate to because they are so inconsistent with their habits and the people that they surround themselves with. They change their behavior depending on who they're with, and that's not a person that can be trusted. Consistency is so important because as you journey along to fulfilling your purpose, you will encounter people of many different statures. There will be people who have major titles and positions, people that have no titles and positions at all, people who can do something for you, and people who can do nothing at all for you. Therefore, it's important for your behavior to be consistent with everyone and not change depending on who you're with. That means not showing favoritism to the one you feel you can benefit the most from and then neglect the one who cannot do anything for you. It proves your motivates are impure and that's not a person of good character that God will trust with His people.

A person of good character is also trustworthy. Trust is absolutely necessary for successful relationships. Without trust, your relationships will not stand the test of time. In fact, they won't stand at all. Trust is the reliability and strength to building relationships with people. If we are not people of trust, God won't be able to depend on us to live out the purposes He created us with.

Those were just a few qualities of a person with good character now let's talk about convictions. Your convictions are firm beliefs that you hold as pertaining to what you believe to be right or wrong. Of course, everyone's convictions are different, and not everyone holds those same beliefs about a thing. However, conviction is not merely the knowledge of what is right or wrong. Many people know that some of the things they do are clearly wrong but continue to do it because they have no conviction about it. So then, what is conviction? The Bible clearly tells us what conviction is in John 16:8, "He will convict the world of sin, and of righteousness, and of judgment." The word convict means to convince someone of the truth. The Holy Spirit is the one who convinces and convicts us of the sin in our lives and our need for the Savior. The more you grow in your relationship with Christ and allow the Holy Spirit to get rid of the things that are not pleasing to God, your convictions become stronger about the things of this world that you might take part in.

As I mentioned earlier, conviction is not merely having a belief of what's right or wrong, because many people know that sin is wrong, yet they have no revelation about it. Having a conviction comes from the Holy Spirit. You choose not to indulge in sin because you realize the severity of that sin against God and you don't want to go against His word. When you are convicted, you become more mindful of how much your sin dishonors and displeases God. You also become aware of actions in your life that may not necessarily be sin, but those actions are not helping to bring you closer to God. If you are to live a life of integrity before God, then you must have godly convictions based on the word of God that is produced by the

Holy Spirit dwelling inside of you and ridding you of those things that dishonor God.

Next, is compromise. Compromise is accepting standards that are lower than desirable. Now, compromise by definition means that you do have certain standards that you uphold in your life. However, for one reason or another you lower those standards. One of the many reasons people compromise their standards is because they are trying to please the world. Of course, we all want to be accepted, but you begin to compromise when your desire to be accepted by the world is greater than your desire to be accepted by God. When the world has a greater influence on your life than the One who gave you life, you're in trouble. Another reason is not believing you have what it takes to fulfill the will of God for your life, so you live a life settling for things that are not His best. Perhaps you have given up on believing the promises of God for your life will come to pass so you once again settle for less than what God has for you. Compromise is probably the greatest problem facing the follower of Christ in this day and age. The more you compromise, the more you move away from the will of God and the purpose He has for your life.

Lastly, integrity is the wholeness or completeness of your character. It's having a high standard of living based on a personal code of honesty and behavior that doesn't give in at a moment of weakness. Let's say your character is who you actually are and your integrity is made up of the continued decisions that you make, based on who you are. It's how you live when no one else is watching you. This is not a matter of perfection, but of honesty without compromise or corruption. So many people make bad decisions in their lives because of their faulty character leading them with no integrity. We see a lack of integrity coupled with compromise so much in the area of relationships and immorality. People make bad decisions and don't set up strong boundaries, so it puts them in situations where they compromise. Without integrity, you'll never be able to carry out the call of God on your life because you will always compromise and forfeit where God is taking you. Gifting's, positions, and titles, do not matter when your integrity is not consistent in your life. You will fail every time. I feel as though integrity is one of the most devalued characteristics that leaders hold today. People care more about popularity and who you know, when they should be more concerned with living a life of integrity before God. Psalm 101:2 reads, "I will be careful to live a blameless life- when will you come to help me? I will lead a life of integrity in my own home." This goes without question that integrity starts in the home of your heart.

Without good character, you won't have strong convictions, which will cause you to compromise every time, and walk without integrity.

Chapter 11
Self-Control

Self-control is literally like an anchor to your soul. It is one of the fruits of the Holy Spirit and it is very important in your journey to fulfilling your purpose. If we do not operate with self-control, we are liable to step out and do the very things that will cause us to risk what we worked so hard for. Having self-control in its simplest form means stopping yourself from doing the things that your flesh wants to do but may not be in your best interest. So many people fall into the temptations of everyday life and do not exercise self-control. Having self-control as it pertains to walking in your purpose means demonstrating it even in the little, everyday decisions that you make. Little decisions, yet they affect you so greatly. There are many areas of self-control that we can talk about, but I want to focus on first, the area of our emotions. This is one of the most important areas in your life where you'll need to exercise self-control. If your emotions are not controlled in the areas I'm going to mention as you continue reading you will literally forfeit or majorly delay what God is calling you to do.

Have you ever heard someone say to you or someone else, "You are so emotional?" It's okay to be emotional because we all are in some way; however, it's not okay for us to be led by our emotions. Our emotions can sometimes play tricks on us. Your emotions and what you feel are very real; however, they may be based off a perception or a situation that is not true. For example, let's assume that one of your friends walk right past you and didn't speak to you today. How would that make you feel? Perhaps ignored or even rejected by that person? Now in actuality, your friend had a lot going on that day and didn't even notice you, as they were consumed with so much and focused on the destination. The truth is that they failed to see outside of where they were going that particular day. So it wasn't that you were being ignored, it's that you weren't seen, and you developed emotions about the situation that caused you to react negatively. All of a sudden, you find yourself now returning what you perceived as a rude gesture, and you make the decision to ignore that person going forward. What you felt was real, but it was based on an inaccurate situation. This is how our emotions can deceive us and cause us to act in a way that is not in our best interest. We see this happen so often to people. That's why it is so important for us not to allow our emotions to control our actions but to step back and take a look at things and say to ourselves, "God how should I react to this going forward?" If we filter our emotions through the Holy Spirit, He will guide us to handle things the best way possible, regardless of whether our perception of a situation is accurate or not.

Along your journey, you will encounter so many people and situations, and you will be given countless opportunities to allow your emotions to cause you to react in a manner that isn't always best for you. So if you allow your emotions to control your actions, you will fail every time and make the wrong decisions. Understand that Jesus also felt some of the same emotions that we feel today; however, you will read all throughout the Scriptures that Jesus was emotional about things that were pertaining to the will of God. He was angry, frustrated, grieved, compassionate and rejected; all of the above, but He did not allow His emotions to cause His actions to be sinful. When you allow your emotions to control your actions in a negative way, it hinders what the Holy Spirit is trying to do in and through you.

Next is exercising self-control in your desires. What do you desire? Of course, we all desire something in life. Desires can be a good thing, but it can also be a bad thing. It just depends on what you desire. I have seen too many great men and women of God falter because their desires were not in alignment with the will of God. 1 John 2:15-17 says, "Do not love the world or things in the world. If anyone loves the world, the love of the

Father is not in him. For all that is in the world- the desires of the flesh and desires of the eyes and pride in possessions- is not from the Father but from the world. And the world is passing away along with its desires, but whoever does the will of God abides forever."

There are three different types of desires described in this passage of Scripture that I want to go in detail with you about. The first one is the desire of the flesh. We are spiritual beings; however, we all have fleshly desires. What I mean by this is, fleshy desires that do not honor the spirit of God and can be sinful. The Bible tells us in Matthew 26:41, "For the spirit is willing, but the flesh is weak." This means that our flesh is constantly doing things contrary to what the Holy Spirit would want to produce in our lives. Galatians 5:17 reads, "For the flesh desires what is contrary to the spirit, and the spirit what is contrary to the flesh. They are in conflict with each other so that you are not to do whatever you want." We live in a world and a time where we're encouraged to just do whatever feels right, but that is not what God desires. This scripture clearly instructs us not to do whatever we want to do, or whatever we personally feel or believe is right. This includes selfish desires that would bring your flesh satisfaction but does not line up with the character of Christ. Fleshly desires such as any sexual or lustful desires that you feel you cannot control, you will need to rely on the Holy Spirit to give you the strength to resist those desires. Since your flesh always wants you to do what goes against the spirit; therefore, you must constantly submit your fleshly desires to God so that you are not controlled by it and led into sin. Sexual sin or fleshly desires is the quickest way to keep us from fulfilling the purpose of God. Galatians 5:19-21, says, "The acts of the flesh are obvious; sexual immorality, impurity, and debauchery, idolatry and witchcraft, hatred did discord, jealousy, outbursts of rage, selfish ambition, dissensions, and in the drunkenness, orgies." When you allow the flesh the very things that you are to submit to God, you are not aligning with what God is trying to do in your life. We are instructed to turn from godless living and sinful pleasures. Titus 2:12, says, "We should live in this evil world with wisdom, righteousness, and devotion to God." You may say that the temptation is too great to deny; however, temptations come from our own desires and our desires come from what's in our heart. James 1:15 reads, "These desires give birth to sinful actions. And when sin is allowed to grow, it gives birth to death." It gives death to your dreams, your vision and to the will of God for your life. So we must first ask God to cleanse our heart of all impurity and unrighteousness so that we no longer desire what's contrary to his Holy Spirit.

Secondly, it talks about the desires of the eyes. This is referring to the desire to possess what we see or have those things that have visual appeal to us. This can be coveting of money, possessions or other physical things that are not from God, but the world. Coveting is an unhealthy desire. Wanting to possess what one has is a spirit of greed. Its basis comes from the discontentment in which one has. It is sinful because it's contrary to being content. It takes your trust and your focus off of God, and it puts your hope in the things of this world. Therefore, we should not covet people or possessions. That's why we see so much adultery or wild living in our world today. It's because we see something that appears to be pleasing to the eye and we want more because we're not content with what we already have. We must be content because wandering eyes will always take you to a place that you didn't bargain for.

Lastly is the desire of pride of life. The pride of life means desiring anything that will lead to pride itself, boasting in arrogance or lifting yourself up. These things are not from God, but of the world. This can mean boasting in your accomplishments or your status in life. Don't misunderstand what I'm saying here; it's okay to be proud of your accomplishments or achievements; however, it becomes prideful when you have an excessively high opinion of yourself because of it. The thing about pride of life is that it gives an illusion of false godlike characters. We mistakenly call it confidence when it's really arrogance. The pride of life is probably the most evil temptation of them all because it seeks to elevate itself above all others and fulfill every personal desire. In the Bible, the prophet Isaiah talks about how Satan wanted to exalt himself above God; he desired to be God instead of His servant. He was puffed up with pride, and it consumed his desires and decisions. Isaiah 14:14, "I will climb to the highest heavens and be like the Most High." Pride is one of the leading causes of strife in your home, within your family, within your church and within yourself. Jesus says we must deny ourselves and take up our cross and follow him, so pride is a direct contradiction to how Christ followers are to live. We must ask God to humble our heart so that we are not controlled by pride.

I believe the tongue is an area that we can all probably say we need self-control as well. Just because you think something, doesn't mean you need to say it. Contrary to what you've heard, everything does not need to be said! Your words can get you in a lot of trouble if you do not tame your tongue. The tongue has incredible power and can bring up blessings or curses or death into your life. The wise hold their tongue and the foolish blurt out whatever they want to say. We've been so trained in life to think, "this is just how I am; I say what I have to say because I like to keep it real." That is stemmed from a foolish heart and not a heart that understands the power of your words and how they may affect a potential situation or person. Sometimes it's better to be quiet in situations of animosity and frustration, because during those times you're not sure what's going to fly out of your mouth, and you want to be wise. Proverbs 21:23 reads, "Those who guard their mouths and their tongues keep themselves from calamity." It really takes a person of maturity and honor to control their tongue. Further more, you want the words you speak to gentle and uplifting. Ephesians 4:29 says, " Don't use foul or abusive language. Let everything you say be good and helpful, so that your words will be an encouragement to those who hear them."

The last area of self-control that I want to talk about is in your finances. You have to learn how to control your finances or spending habits. God's desire is for us to be good stewards of our money. Now be honest, are you someone who loves to shop, spend money, and impulsively buy things? I don't want to give you the wrong perception of money because there's nothing wrong with money. We all know that to live in this life we must have money. In fact, Solomon says in Ecclesiastes 10:19 that "money answers everything." So there is nothing wrong with having money. Many people were brought up thinking that money is evil and not from God; however, that is not true. The Bible says in 1 Timothy 6:10 that, "the LOVE of money is the root of all evil." So when you make money your god, is when it becomes a problem. Because you can't serve both God and money, you'll love one and hate the other. God wants you to manage your finances properly so that it will bear fruit and grow.

So why should we have self-control in our finances and be good stewards of our money? Because we must remember we're not just living for today or for the moment, rather, we are also living for tomorrow. I will give you five reasons in which being a good steward of the money God has given you is important.

1. It allows you to first and foremost tithe. Your tithe is your first 10% that is used towards building the kingdom of God.
2. It allows you to save for your future. You don't want to live paycheck to paycheck and have nothing to show for it. You want to make sure that with every penny you get you put some aside for yourself and for your tomorrow.
3. It allows you to pay off any possible debt you may have. Debt is when you are in obligation to someone else. So you want to free yourself from being obligated to anyone. When you are a good steward of your money, you can tithe, save, and also use your money to pay off debt.
4. It allows you to invest in your future. You can buy for the things that you actually need and not just want, such as a home, a car or even investing in businesses.
5. Last but definitely not least it allows you to be able to give. It is better to give than to receive. Being a good steward of your money

positions you to be able to give and help others. We can give to those in need; we can give to missions, as well as other projects that advance the kingdom of God. But we can also use our finances to fund the vision that God has put on our own hearts.

Having self-control in all these areas is so crucial to us moving in alignment to what God wants to do in us and through us. Having self-control is a mark of maturity and growth in Christ.

Chapter 12
Forgiveness

Looking at me and talking with me today, you might find it hard to believe that for many years, pain and hurt consumed me. As a child, I had been through many traumatic experiences that shaped my life and caused me to see everything through eyes of hurt, rejection, and disappointment. The ones who should have loved me most were only shadows of what they could have been in my life. The lack of love that I should have been shown in my life caused me to carry around so much pain. Unfortunate circumstances led to me being taken away from my biological family at the age of three. As young as I was, I still remember the clouds of smoke that surrounded me from cigarettes, and being left at different houses, while my parents were out doing God knows what, with God knows who. I remember being exposed to a life that was unsuitable for a child, especially one of my age. Soon, I was placed in a foster home away from the only family I knew. That was the last memory I had of my family. No calls, no visits, nothing but shadows without faces. There was a court case later when I was around the age of seven for my mom to get custody of me. I remember being so excited to hear when I would see my family again, but I was scarred with hearing these words, "I don't want them." I remember thinking to myself. "How could they not want me? How could they not want their first-born child? I didn't ask to be born." It created feelings of unwantedness within me. It hurt me to the core and I bottled everything up not wanting to talk about it. I unknowingly built walls as a means to protect myself from anyone hurting me again. I could not move forward from the hurt that plagued me, and it made me angry at the thought of it. It made me angry towards those who caused the pain. I later realized that I was harboring unforgiveness in my heart. But what is forgiveness? What did that truly mean? I'm sure you've also heard that you must forgive, but what does that look like in your life?

Unforgiveness is holding a grudge against someone who has hurt, wronged or offended you in some way. It's not having the compassion to forgive them. While you may find it hard to forgive that person, I want you to know that satan's attempt is to destroy that relationship. If you do not have compassion in your heart for a person that God still has compassion for, then you have given power to satan in your life. I want you to think about it. Who is that person in your life that has hurt or offended you? The person who, at the thought of them, makes you cringe. Yes, that person, God still loves them. Unforgiveness is a poison that sucks the life right out of you. It hurts you and only you.

I believe that unforgiveness is one of the biggest schemes of satan to destroy your relationships with God and others. It's a sin, and sin separates us from God. God created us to be in fellowship with Him, and unforgiveness hinders that relationship.

2 Corinthians 5:18-19 says, "All this is from God, who reconciled us to himself through Christ and gave us the ministry of reconciliation: that God was reconciling the world to himself in Christ, not counting people's sins against them." God doesn't count your sins against you, but you operate out of the wrong heart when you hold others sin against them. Can you see how Satan is at work to separate us from God and others?

I always felt a sense of rejection from my biological family that made me want them to feel that same sense of rejection that I carried; therefore, I did not have a relationship with my family for most of my life. Satan used that in my life to break the relationship I could have had with my family. Take a look into your life; can you see how he is doing the same thing with you and your loved ones? Satan will use the actions of others to create offense in your life to destroy the relationships that we were meant to have. You may have been betrayed or abandoned by a mother or father. Maybe they should have been there for you, and they weren't. Perhaps you were verbally or physically abused, and it left you scarred. Like myself, you may feel like they didn't care or love you enough to choose a different life that would have included you. Perhaps you had a really bad marriage that ended in divorce, and you feel like your spouse didn't fight for you and it hurt you. Maybe you had a never-ending story of betrayal, and you are unable to trust again. A close friend left you in your darkest time of need. The church disappointed you and let you down. The examples of how others have offended you could go on and on. I truly understand that it hurts to think about the situations that you have encountered. The mere thought of it grips you in terror and fear and causes you to relive the painful experiences all over again. You have allowed the pain to become a part of you, and to break free from it seems to be more painful than not confronting it at all. It feels like a part of your heart is being ripped out of you, and you choose not to experience a greater pain than what caused it in the first place. In not confronting these issues, it leads to you not being able to trust others and sometimes even God because, how could He allow you to go through this, right? You are hurt by others and choose not to forgive them. You turn from God because you feel like He failed you also. Quite the contrary, God loves us and gave His only Son for us because we offended Him with our sin. The thing about God is that He never counts our sin against us. His love for us never changes. He is constantly pursuing us and wants us in relationship with Him. Nothing that anyone can do to you can ever compare to the hurt you caused God after He gave everything for you. What a gracious God. Ephesians 4: 32 say's, "Be kind and compassionate to one another, forgiving each other, just as in Christ God forgave you." I am not saying the pain you've experienced isn't justified. What I am saying is you have the power to forgive others because Christ first forgave you of a far greater debt. You can choose to forgive others and no longer be a victim of your past.

How do you forgive?

1. You must be willing to confront and talk about what caused unforgiveness in your life. You will never forgive if you don't decide to let go and be free. There is healing in opening up about what you have buried in your heart. As long as you keep everything bottled up, it will only fester. What is rooted in your heart will only grow into your life. The decisions you make will be made out of a tainted view of hurt. You must allow unforgiveness to be uprooted from your life. Forgiveness is making a conscious decision to cancel that offense. Find some trusted men or women that you can talk to and you are sure to feel a measure of freedom in your life.

2. Allow God to heal you. I know it's painful and that's why you shouldn't carry this any longer. God wants your pain and your hurt. He wants all of you. He wants you to come to Him and lay it all at His feet so He can heal your heart and emotions. Know that you have a God that will take your pain, so let Him do so.

3. Depend on the Holy Spirit. It is the power of the Holy Spirit that helps us forgive. It's too great of a burden, and you can't do it on your own. It's not a matter of your mind or will, but it's the work of the Holy Spirit in your heart.

4. Choose to forgive. Say the person's name and say out loud, "I forgive you." You must understand that forgiveness is for you and not the other person. It holds you in bondage and captive to your offender. I too had a choice to make in my own life to forgive. I realized unforgiveness held me in bondage from moving forward while forgiveness was a gateway to my heart allowing the love of God to take root.

5. Pray. Think of all those that hurt or offended you and write their names down. Begin to pray for them. Nothing shifts your heart for a person more than praying for them does. Pray for their well-being and that God would bring revelation to them. In doing so refrain from speaking evil of them.

Unforgiveness is a poison that permeates your heart and entire life. Choose forgiveness today and no longer give satan control in your life. God paid a price too high for you. Choose to forgive and allow God to free you that His love would take root in your heart.

Chapter 13
Surrender

When you hear the word surrender, what comes to your mind? Is it something negative? Perhaps you are not sure how you feel when you hear that word? I believe many people would relate it to something negative because by definition you give up control of yourself. In battle, it is also a sign that one has given up any hope for victory. As human beings, we naturally want to be in control of our lives, especially since most of our lives, our parents have exercised control until we become adults. But why do we feel the need to be in control? I believe that for many of us, it makes us feel like our choices or our actions make a difference. We believe our own efforts determine what happens in our lives. The thought of having someone else control or determine the outcome of our life seems almost ridiculous and goes against our nature.

I remember this one particular day like it was yesterday. A series of events took place on that unforgettable evening in 2016. What was supposed to be a nice evening hanging with my home girls, turned into a dreadful night. The night was dark out; however, we had some light from the street post as we walked through the parking lot of the movie theatre. It was myself and two other friends. We all drove in separate cars because we met each other there. The plan was to stop by whichever friends' car was closest parked and then give the others a ride to their cars. As we walked to the car, we talked about the movie we'd just seen and then on to another conversation. The conversation was so good that by the time we made it to the first car we stood beside it, still engaged. Not intentionally, but we all stood at different angles so we could see each other's face as we talked. Out of my friend's peripheral view, she noticed a guy walking to his car. It would appear as though it's nothing out of the ordinary right? However, the puzzled look on my friend's face didn't sit well with me and made me turn in that direction to look. We then saw three other guys coming from different directions that made it look like they were closing in on us. Something just didn't seem quite right about the situation, and terror gripped our hearts. My friend fumbled to get the keys out of her purse so we could finally get into her car just to be on the safe side. While we rushed to get into the car the four guys charged toward us. I wasn't sure if these guys had weapons on them or not, but I didn't want to find out. We didn't quite make it into the car before they approached us. As we were being attacked, several things ran through my mind. I literally thought we were going to die that day and my life flashed before my eyes. I couldn't fathom being resistant at that moment. I was so terrified that all I could think about was giving them whatever they wanted. In the midst of all that was going on I heard a voice say, "just surrender," and at that moment they ran away. Now, I'm very aware that I could have lost my life at that moment, whether I had given them whatever they wanted or not. Of course everyone's reaction could have been different. Some would have tried to fight there way through, while other's would have chosen to try and run. However, in this particular story my decision to surrender spared my life.

What exactly does surrender mean? Surrender means to yield ownership of, to relinquish control over what we consider ours, whether it is our belongings, our time, or our rights.

Truth be told, you surrender all the time. When you get behind the wheel of a car, you are saying that you entrust your life behind the mechanics of this vehicle to get you where you need to be. When you go into the doctor's office for a procedure, you trust that the doctor knows what they are doing and will bring about the best results or desired outcome. So why is it so easy to surrender to these things in everyday life but when it comes to God it becomes difficult. Have you ever thought about it that way? We will sit on an airplane and trust the pilot with our life but not the God that created us. Why? Because it's easier to surrender to something we can see than something or someone that we can't see. If

I trust the pilot, I know that shortly I'll reach my destination, but with God, you are not sure if things will turn out the way you expected, in the time you expect it. So you trust your time and your control better. This is a problem I myself identify with too well. We don't believe that Jesus is all satisfying. We do not think that the joy in Him will surpass anything that we will give up. We do not trust that His ways are higher and His will for our lives is best. God wants us to come to Him, so He can lead us to complete freedom, joy, safety and abundant life.

Romans 12:1-2, says, "Therefore, I urge you, brothers and sisters, in view of God's mercy, to offer your bodies as a living sacrifice, holy and pleasing to God-this is your true and proper worship. Do not conform to the pattern of this world, but be transformed by the renewing of your mind. Then you will be able to test and approve what God's will is-his good, pleasing and perfect will."

If you want a change in your life, if you want complete peace and joy, then God tells you that you must surrender everything to Him.

You must first surrender your mind to God. When you surrender your mind that means you're giving up control of the way you think. So much of the world has influenced how we think since childhood, and it shapes how we behave. Statistics show that television, music, movies, magazines and different types of media shape how we think and act. We let our minds get saturated with violence, false love, indecency, sex, and so many other things. We see violence amongst each other; shootings in schools, inappropriate speech and behavior, sex outside of marriage and the list goes on. When we see these things, it corrupts our perspective of a healthy and godly viewpoint. For example, it appears as if ninety percent of all relationships on television allude to sex outside of marriage and that gives a false perception of love, and it devalues marriage. Therefore we have a tainted understanding of what love is when it pertains to God, who is indeed love. Your mind stores everything you see, hear, and what you remember influences what you do. The Bible says in

Philippians 4:8, "Whatsoever things are true and honest and just and pure and lovely, think on these things." You must allow God to transform the way you think through the washing of the Word so that your thoughts will align with Him. What mindset or thoughts are influencing your life today that you need to surrender to God? If you want your life to change, then your mind must be surrendered to God and transformed.

You must also surrender your body to God. We hear in the world today that our bodies are our own and we can do with it what we please. That is actually not true at all.

1 Corinthians 3:16, says, "Do you not know that you are the temple of God and that the Spirit of God dwells in you?" Our bodies belong to the Lord, that's why we shouldn't do whatever we want with them. We have been taught to do whatever feels good or feels right. Though we have natural desires, it's not best to allow your body to be subjected to anything that is not God's will. Yes, God created sex. However, He planned it from the beginning to be shared with your spouse in the confines of marriage. Casual sex is never really casual. There is a huge cost of broken hearts, broken relationships, bodies and families and God wants to protect us from that.

The Bible says in 1 Corinthians 6:18-20, "Flee from sexual immorality. No other sin so clearly affects the body as this one does. For sexual immorality is a sin against your own body. Don't you realize that your body is the temple of the Holy Spirit who lives in you and was given to you by God? You do not belong to yourself, for God bought you with a high price. So you must honor God with your body." I know that everyone is tempted, but it's not until you surrender to the temptation that it becomes sin in your life. You must surrender your body to God and allow the Holy Spirit to give you strength not to fall or put yourself in situations to dishonor God with your body. You may say, "I've already given myself in this area" so it's too late for me. God is gracious and forgiving. He seeks to restore and rebuild His people. It's never too late.

You must also surrender your will to God. Luke 22:42, says, "Father, if you are willing, take this cup from me, yet not my will, but yours be done." Despite what Jesus wanted or felt, He wanted the will of His Father more. This passage of scripture is right before the crucifixion was about to take place in Jesus' life. He knew that it would be painful, but He knew it would be more painful not submitting to God's plan. I'm not saying surrendering your will is going to be easy. As a matter of fact, I can assure you that there might be some painful experiences along the way, but the glory in surrendering to God despite those difficult moments brings everlasting rewards. I get it, we don't want to feel the pain of relinquishing our will to God, but when you realize this world has nothing to offer you in comparison to God, the decision becomes easier. God's perfect will is always better and everything that comes along with it. You must be willing to allow the Lord to lead every aspect of your life.

You must also surrender your heart to God. The heart is what God is after. Jeremiah 17:9 reads, "The human heart is the most deceitful of all things, and desperately wicked. Who really knows how bad it is?" We must allow the Lord to give us a new heart. He has to transform your heart so that He can take root and grow in your heart. The notion to "just follow your heart" can be very deceiving if it's not surrendered to God because it can lead us astray every time. From the heart is where everything else flows from pertaining to life. Matthew 15:19, says, "For from the heart come evil thoughts, murder, adultery, all sexual immorality, theft, lying, and slander." Everything you do and say is stemmed from what lies in your heart. God must rid us of all ungodliness so that our hearts' desires are to please Him.

God loves us immensely. He wants our heart so that He can heal it, repair it, transform it and mold it so that His love can take root. You must be willing to surrender your life to God if you want to fulfill His purpose for your life

Chapter 14
Intentional Friendships

It was my eighth-grade year and I'd just moved to Upper Marlboro, Maryland, where I didn't know anyone. Before this, I had lived in Fort Washington, MD. Here I was, an early adolescent becoming a young lady, and I was experiencing one of the greatest changes in my life. New house, new school and that meant I wouldn't know anyone around the neighborhood or at my school. As a young girl, I never had a problem making friends; however, I quickly realized and understood that having good friends was going to be my greatest challenge.

I'll never forget standing there with my mom in the registration office of my middle school registering for school. It was the summer time and in walks another girl who asked me, "Are you new here?" Assuming she was new also, I immediately said, "YES!" That was the beginning of a beautiful friendship. Up until that point in my life, I never questioned the thought of what a friend should look like or how a friend should behave.

She introduced herself to me and later became my closest and dearest friend throughout middle school and high school; in fact, she and I are still close friends today. I would say that she pursued me; she instantly connected with me in a way that no one else had before. She knew my likes, dislikes, and love language even before that was a thing. I loved going over to her house and hanging out with her and her family and eating up all their snacks. She even knew my favorite snack, the Little Debbie brownies, and she would make sure she always had some at home.

I remember the first time I went over to her house after school one day. We rode the yellow school bus, and upon approaching her stop, she said, "This is it; let's go." I proceeded to walk to the exit doors. I turned around and saw that she was still sitting in her seat, laughing with the others on the bus, and even though I was so embarrassed, I thought to myself, "I really like this girl." She made me appreciate the little things in life. She was the type of friend that made you wonder if you ever had real friends in the first place.

When I graduated from high school and moved to Baton Rouge, Louisiana for college I knew I had to start all over again. Once again, I didn't know anyone, and no one knew me. Though I always had my dearest friend in my heart, she was not physically with me in college. I was entering adulthood and knew I needed some meaningful relationships. Thankfully, my friend had spent the last five years of my life laying out for me what I should look for in a friend. It is true that as we grow and mature we do become wiser and our elementary concepts of how life works tend to change. When I look back over my life and the many, great friendships that I've made during that time, it's clear to me that most of them were intentional. In this chapter, I'm going to break down exactly what it means to be intentional when it comes to forming friendships and how having unintentional friendships will hinder your purpose in life while having intentional friendships will propel you toward your life's purpose.

When we think about friendships, we usually think of people who have been there for us the longest, or people we can talk to and have fun with. Though none of that is wrong, we must begin to look at friendships from a different point of view. Keep in mind, we all have our own definition of what we think a friend is or should be. Webster's dictionary defines a friend as a person whom one knows and with whom one has a bond of mutual affection. Now, perhaps that definition is very broad and doesn't give much insight as to what a friend really is, so allow me to shine a little more light on the subject. We can share a mutual affection for many people, but that doesn't mean we will walk with and do life with every one of those people. There has to be some distinct characteristics that set a person apart. We will look at some of those characteristics a little later in this chapter.

To really understand intentional friendships we have to look at what the words intentional and friendship means? Our definition of intentional friendships will shape how strong of relationships we have in our lives. So let's break down what it means to be intentional in the friendships we pursue or the friendships that pursue us. Don't get me wrong, as stated before, not every single relationship in your life will be intentional. Some relationships happen because of life circumstances. Let's take your place of employment for example; you have to work with your associates on the job. In school, you don't choose the people that are in your class or who your group partner will be. These relationships may be circumstantial; however, they can become intentional. I actually have a particular friend comes to mind. I had just started working with a new company, and they sat me right beside her, so we inevitably began talking from day to day. Over time our bond got stronger as we began to share more intimate details of our life. There was a trust and openness that made the relationship more meaningful. We would talk about life, family, growing closer to God, and would even occasionally pray together. We discovered that we'd come from somewhat similar backgrounds and shared emotions that came with our experiences. God began putting her on my heart more each day, and I began to ask God what should I pray for her about. God made it very clear that there is a purpose in our friendship. I am pretty intentional with the relationships I pursue, but to be honest, that friendship came about unexpectedly. So that relationship started off circumstantial but became very intentional and is now one of my dearest friendships. However, if you are not intentional in your friendships, you can possibly end up with purposeless relationships in your life.

Intentional means done with purpose, or deliberately planned with the expectation of specific results. You have to intentionally seek out the friends you want in your life. The first intentional friendship we should all seek in our lives is one with God. He is a friend to the friendless and sticks closer than a brother. Let's go through some character traits that we see displayed in God when it comes to being a good friend:

- *He is all loving.* He loves us unconditionally, and there is nothing we can do to separate us from His love. His love for you is not based on what you do. It's not fickle, pending on circumstances or conditions. It's everlasting. We can take comfort in knowing that His love never fails.

- *He is sacrificial.* Sacrifice sees something and considers that thing to be worth whatever the cost is. He considered you worth it, and because of love, He paid the highest price possible - giving His only Son, Jesus Christ. There is no sacrifice without love. When you truly love someone, you will sacrifice for him or her. God gave His most precious gift – bankrupting all of Heaven for you.

- *He is patient.* God is so patient in that He gives us time here on Earth that we don't deserve. A thousand years is like a day to the Lord. While we live our lives here on earth, doing what we want to do, God still allows time for us to turn to Him.

- *He is faithful.* Even when we aren't faithful to God He remains faithful to us. His word says He cannot deny himself.

- *He is trustworthy.* The Bible says the decrees of the Lord are trustworthy. We can see all throughout the Bible that God stands behind His word. You can look at your life knowing that God is there because you wake up every morning. You can trust God because His word is proven true.

- *He is loyal.* God is wholeheartedly committed to you. He established loyalty through his covenant relationship: "Know therefore that the Lord your God is God, the faithful God who maintains loyalty with those who love Him and keep His commandments, to a thousand generations" – Deuteronomy 7:9.

This list is not intended to be a fully exhausted list of all of the characteristics of God. However, I wanted to highlight a handful of the attributes of God that I felt were most important and that you can begin using immediately in your own life. Though God is perfect in all of His ways, we are not, and should seek to possess these traits daily. So we can say a friend is one who is loving, sacrificial, patient, faithful, trustworthy, and loyal.

Now let's look at the traits of friends we should intentionally seek to walk in fellowship with. I'll mention some things that might be hard for you to hear because it's not common in this day.

- *Truthful and honest.* "Wounds from a sincere friend are better than kisses from an enemy"- Proverbs 27:6. Your friends should be people who can tell you the truth about yourself even if it hurts because they love you. A friend who only tells you what you want to hear does not have your best interest at heart and does you a disservice. A friend will help you see the "ugly" in your life and help you to avoid trying to blame everyone else. People aren't use to wounds from friends because all their friends have ever done is kiss them and try to make them feel good. Just to be clear, this passage isn't saying that your friends should be people who purposely try to hurt you rather, they should be people who love you enough to help you see what needs to change in your life. They can call you out and hold you accountable when your actions are not at their best. Have friends in your life that when you rant about a situation they say, "No, that was actually your fault, go apologize," or help you see what you could have done or said differently to produce a better outcome. I was recently telling one of my friends about a situation, and she said, "You are being ridiculous and dramatic." I stopped, and my natural reaction was to hang the phone up and the next day, tell her it was a bad signal. My next thought was to say, "Who do you think you are talking to?" Her comment totally caught me off guard, but I appreciated it because she didn't allow me to believe that what I said made sense. Good friends, real friends, are those who will undoubtedly have your best interest at heart and tell you in love what you need to hear versus what you want to hear.

- *Sharpens you.* "As iron sharpens iron, so a friend sharpens a friend." – Proverbs 27:17. When two blades rub together, sparks begin to fly everywhere, and the edges actually become sharper. It makes the blade more efficient in its task. When you and your friends come together, you should help each other become more efficient in your purpose. You should feel encouraged and empowered to fulfill your dreams, passions, and goals after being around your friends. Something inside of your friends should cause your purpose to leap with excitement and fire you up about fulfilling the things God has in store for you. If the blade is dull, it won't really be useful and accomplish its intended purpose so make sure your friends sharpen you in a way that pushes you closer to your God-given purpose.

- *Accountability and vulnerability.* This is one of the most important things to have in your life and friendships. I see a culture where no one understands what this really means and therefore it is tremendously lacked. People are going throughout life, and though people may surround them, they are not sharing their temptations and struggles with anyone to help them avoid dangerous pitfalls. Accountability is giving an account or being honest to someone about your temptations, desires, and struggles. Now I want to assure you that this is not a bad thing. It's actually a great thing and it's something that you should desire to seek out. Not only is it a good idea to be accountable to a friend, but it's also biblical. The Bible tells us in James 5:16 to, "Confess your trespasses to one another, and pray for one another, that you may be healed." There is nothing greater than a friend who will walk with you, pray with you and be there for you no matter what you're going through and not judge you. Having friends to keep you accountable is not just about confronting you when you're doing or saying things that you know you shouldn't say or do but more about helping you avoid ungodly behavior, unwise choices, and dangerous temptations in your life. You want to have a friend that is close enough to know your intimate struggles so they can celebrate your triumphs with you and uplift you during your weaknesses. These friends are not easy to come by. It's also important to understand that it takes time to cultivate these relationships to where you feel comfortable with giving that high level of access to your life. I've seen the effects of people who have accountability and those who don't and simply put; accountability will save your life. I have friends that have complete access into my life. They can speak into my life and give constructive criticism, and I know it's coming from a place of genuine love because I totally trust them. The thing about this is not having anything to hide. When you want to live a life of purpose and set a godly example before men, you desire to share your life with a close friend because you don't want to fall into the snares of the enemy. When I have an internal struggle or temptation I immediately tell my friends because I don't want my thoughts to turn into actions. It is imperative that you find a friend that you can be accountable with. Vulnerability is often looked at as a negative thing because it creates a great level of exposure in our lives. Our human nature doesn't want people to know what we deal with or struggle with. We think that by avoiding being vulnerable to people is a sign of strength, but it's actually the exact opposite. It takes much more strength to be vulnerable than it does to keep ourselves protected. You have to be vulnerable and allow the walls to come down or you'll crack one day. You need friends that you can trust to help share your burdens with and will cover you. This is one of the things I value most in friendship, knowing that you are not alone and you have someone there to share with you what you are going through. Being a good friend isn't just about being there for someone else, but it's also about allowing a friend to be there for you.

- *Transparency and openness.* Transparency is intentionally baring your soul to the world by showing your true self to others. I'm reminded of Romans 8:19, "For the earnest expectation of the creature waits for the manifestation of the sons of God." This is saying that the world is ready and waiting, in great expectation for you to show up as your true self. This is why transparency is so important! The more you hide your true self, the more you become someone you were never meant to be. Your life becomes disgruntled because you're living as someone God never created you to be. However, you hide your true self for fear of being rejected or disappointed in yourself. Your lack of confidence in yourself gives you a false sense of security in being someone that you are not. The reality is that, all of this is only making matters worse for you the longer you live outside of your authentic self. You need a friend that you can be truly transparent with and allow them to really see you for who you are. Transparency is when you willingly share your life with those you trust. I heard a great man say one day, that openness is being honest about something when asked, but being transparent is voluntarily offering the information.

- *Share common values.* Values are personal beliefs that come from within, deciding right from wrong or what's important. What is right or wrong or important for one person may differ for the next. Now, I'm not disputing whether a person is right or wrong for their values here. I'm merely pointing out that it can cause conflict if the values that you have for your personal life are not commonly shared with your friends. Equally important is valuing what is important to your friend. For example, if I am your friend, and you communicate to me that you highly value your family, then your family will be very important to me, even if I have never met them. This goes the same with lifestyle choices. I'm not saying you have to be the same person, but you should be of one heart and one mind sharing common interests. If your core values are not shared, you can find that friendship more frustrating than rewarding.

- *Celebrates you.* We live in a generation where jealousy is so prevalent. People want to rise to the top and don't care who they step on in the process. You want friends that celebrate your highs and walk with you during your lows. You want people that are genuinely happy for you, even if it doesn't happen for them. I've heard it said, you want people to celebrate you not tolerate you. People that are going to be in your corner no matter what happens, rain or shine. You want friends that will genuinely share in your joys.

I believe these are some essential characteristics to seek out to make your friendships more intentional. You have to be open to the fact that someone else may also be seeking this type of friend as well. I would always say, " I choose my friends, they don't choose me." That way I was in control of the types of relationships I had in my life. But I had to realize it's not always about the relationships I have in my life, but it's also about the relationship someone else may need in their life. There was a time in my life that I had a young lady who was pursuing my friendship. I didn't realize it at the time, but God always has a way of revealing certain things to us. She would call, text, and always wanted to hang out. I was not very open to it; I already had enough friends in my life. I don't believe in surface level friendships, and this person seemed like she just wanted to hang out. She did not particularly want to hang out with the crowd I wanted to be around. I confided in a close friend and told her the situation. I mentioned how I didn't want to be rude to the other girl, plus I didn't need any more friends. She said these words that changed my perspective, "Maybe she needs you." I saw the situation differently that day. It completely changed the way I approached how I would choose my friends from then on.

Some relationships fade over time, and that's okay because they were probably not intentionally formed.   However, other friendships will last a lifetime no matter the distance, or season of life you're in because it was intentionally built. However, no matter how long our friendships last, we should always strive to be the kind of friend that we seek in others.

Section Three:

DEPLOY

Chapter 15
Have a Vision

In this chapter, I am going to distinguish the difference between having sight and having vision. It's been my experience that people often confuse the two and therefore unable to effectively put into practice in their lives. For those of us who have been blessed to have physical sight, we can thank God every day for our ability to SEE with our natural eye; however, we can be spiritually blind, causing us not to be able to PERCEIVE - in the spirit - what the Lord is trying to show us. What God is showing you in the spirit is what I refer to as vision. Having vision is so important to the process of you fulfilling your purpose.

In order to better understand the differences between sight and vision, let's first look at what sight is. It's actually quite simple, sight is having the ability to see something with your natural eye. I refer to the natural as compared to the spiritual quite often because there is a difference between the two, and the Bible makes references to both. There's a clear distinction between the two words. There are times in the Bible where Jesus talks about giving sight to physically blind eyes. And there are also times in the Bible where it talks about people who are without vision is perishing. Proverbs 29:18 says, "Where there is no vision the people perish, but he that keeps the law happy is he." So without a vision, we are not only dying eternally but also our life can be unhappy as well. This is why so many people exist every day and yet feel dead, empty, and miserable on the inside. Have you ever experienced a time in your life when you felt unfulfilled, yet you knew that there was more to the life you were living? Perhaps you feel that way today. You should know that God intends for your life to not only have meaning and significance, but He desires to reveal to you in the spirit what His plans are and what He needs you to do, as well as how He needs you to do it.

One of the worst feelings you can ever experience in your life is being able to see something but not being able to perceive or understand what's going on. For example, my family absolutely hates watching movies with me, because even though we're all watching the same thing, if something happens that I don't understand, I ask questions seeking a better understanding. All they can say to me in those moments is, "Just watch." Even though I'm seeing the same thing my family is seeing, my understanding is not reaching what their understanding is reaching. At times, I can get so frustrated when that happens because naturally, the human mind wants to understand things that are going on around them. Therefore, it causes us to keep asking questions in our boggled minds until it clicks, and we have the understanding we are so desperately seeking.

Therefore, vision goes beyond the ability to simply see. Vision has to do with your ability to perceive or become aware of something. Vision is your ability to realize or comprehend what the Lord is doing. Vision comes from the Lord opening up your understanding concerning his direction for your life. The Scripture says, "Where there is no vision, the people perish: but he that keeps the law, happy is he."- Proverbs 29:18. When God begins to open up your understanding of His word, things become clearer in your life, vision is cast, and purpose can begin to be realized.

I was intentional in discussing what purpose is in a previous chapter because before we can talk about having a vision, we need to first understand what your purpose is. Purpose is the foundation of your vision; it's the source of your vision. I would encourage you to go back and read what I've written in the chapter on purpose in this book because it's going to be very critical that you see how all of this works together. Christ is the foundation for knowing who you are and having a vision for your life. It can become easy for us to struggle with vision when we don't know what our purpose in life is. Once you know your purpose, it's easier for you to receive a vision for your life. It's very important that you realize and understand who you are in Christ. What's your true identity? By spending time in prayer and in the word of God, He will begin to reveal to you exactly who you are in Him. This will give you the answers to your identity that you've been searching for. He will confirm who you are and affirm you as His own. There's no greater feeling in the world than knowing who you are. When you understand your identity, you can be sure of yourself, confident in life. You can walk with your head up. You stop doubting and questioning how you should walk, talk, behave, and approach life. Instead, you become confident in everything that you do. You develop a sense of absolute certainty that can't be shaken. By understanding your identity, you're able to receive your purpose. Many people have a hard time receiving their purpose in life simply because they doubt themselves. They have not yet discovered and accepted who they are in Christ. They have yet to believe who God says they are. Settle your identity in your heart, and soon you will be able to see clearly enough to receive the purpose that God has for your life. And as I've said, your purpose is the foundation for your vision. God gives you identity so that He can provide you with purpose. But you need a way or a plan that will show you how you will accomplish your purpose. This is your vision. It's a trifactor: all three working together. None can work independently of the other, and it will always come in this order: Identity, Purpose, and Vision.

When I understood my purpose was to raise up women to be healed and delivered by the power of God, to see their minds free from the shackles of the enemy, and to see them knowing who they are in the Lord, I began to actually see it happening in the spiritual realm. I began to see myself helping women all over the world, speaking and equipping them to know who they are and to fulfill their destiny. When you begin to see what you were born to do that's a vision. God then began to order my steps and give me ideas and a plan to see that vision come to pass, and I am confident that He will do the same for you. All you have to do is see it. Vision motivates you to reach those goals and get what's required of you done because you can perceive what God is going to do through this.

Chapter 16
Have a Plan

I tell my friends every year that you have to write out a plan for your life. I know it sounds cliché and mundane, but it's so beneficial to you. People without a plan are aimlessly living life with the expectation of something great happening instead of planning for something great to happen. Things don't just fall into our lap; we have to plan and execute. Here are a few reasons why having a plan is so important to your success.

Plans are your outline or steps you take to achieve your goals. So I guess the best thing to do here is back up and talk about goals. Goals are your desired vision of where you want to be. Goals are great because it gives us something to work towards; however, goals must be measurable. There has to be something to measure whether or not you are meeting that goal. A goal that cannot be measured is just an idea. For example, if I say my goal is to eat healthier. Well, how can I measure that I'm eating healthier? My plan to eat healthier is to eliminate processed foods and sweets. I can measure that goal by knowing whether I'm eating processed foods and sweets or not. So a plan is actually the action steps that you are taking to reach and measure your goals.

Back in February of 2013 I moved to Houston, Texas. This new and big city was quite different than where I'd moved from in Baton Rouge Louisiana. But God had put on my heart to host spiritual retreats for women. That had always been my heart, but it was so easy for me to see that happen in Baton Rouge because there was a system already set up in place for that to happen at my church. Moving to Texas was quite different because I didn't know one lady I could start with. I needed a plan. I sat on this vision for years because I never put a plan together; I never took action on what God placed in my heart. It wasn't until 2018, yes five years later that the Lord said "you shall sit on this no longer" and I couldn't ignore it. I began to plan a women's retreat, and then I executed it. I planned everything out to the T, and it was a great success. So even though God had put that on my heart, God was not going to do it for me. I needed a plan to execute the things that God had given me. As you see without that plan, I sat on that vision for five long years. So many of you are the same way, you have things in your heart you desire to do, but you sit on it year after year because you never put a plan together and therefore your dreams die on the inside of you.

Having a plan helps you to prioritize what's important in your life. We all know that prioritizing is key. Because you don't want to spend most of your time on something insignificant when your time should be dedicated to something greater. You learn to focus on the things that will set you up for your future.

Having a plan also allows you to see what you need to say "no" to. Sometimes saying no can be very hard I do understand because I used to be one of those people. It was so hard for me to say no because I didn't want to hurt anyone's feelings or make them feel like they weren't important to me, but I had to learn that was not the case. There are so many things that you will not be able to do and that you just cannot do. Not everyone will understand that, but YOU have to understand that. When you have a certain vision in mind that you are trying to see come to pass there are things and people in your life that may not fit along the lines of what God is calling you to do, and that's okay. So when you prioritize the things in your life that are most important does that thing fit in with it. I'm by no means saying people aren't important, I'm saying you must learn which calls can wait until later. Nor am I saying that you just turn people down if they need your help. What I am saying is this, other people will not understand what you are doing if they are not like-minded. No one will value your time or plans the way you do. And if you don't establish what to say "no" to, you will be tossed to and fro and not fulfill your plans. To say no to someone is not being mean to them, what it's actually doing is setting up boundaries for your life. Boundaries are good because God has set up boundaries for us through his word and we should also set up boundaries for our life as well. To be honest, some things just aren't worth our time. Some things can wait until later. When it became an interference with my purpose God taught me how to say no real quick. And when I say no it was never in a rude manner but in a way that led them to see that this can wait.

Having a plan also helps you to conquer the fear of failure. I've talked to several people just this year alone, and they told me that they don't set goals. When I asked why they said because if I don't reach it then at least I didn't fail. In fact, as stated by Benjamin Franklin, "If you fail to plan, you plan to fail." That led me to see that people fear not meeting their goals. However, as I mentioned earlier, to not have a plan is to aimlessly live life in the expectation that something great will happen instead of making something great happen. So many people do not meet their goals because they do not have a plan for it or the accountability to keep them on track. If you set up a well thought out plan and have people in your life to keep you accountable, then it is possible for you to reach every goal or fulfill what God has placed in your heart. My greatest sadness in life is not seeing people fulfill all that God has called them to be or that he has put in their hearts to do. So I will push for people to set up an action plan to see their dreams come to pass.

So here are a few steps below to help you understand what it means to have a plan and how to execute it.

1. Set measurable goals. Remember a goal that cannot be measured is just an idea. EX. My goal is drawing closer to God this year.
2. Measurable: I will read my bible every day and go to church consistently.

3. Set your plan. I will wake up every day at 6:30 AM and spend 20 minutes reading my Bible and praying. With this, I will be in bed at a reasonable time, so I won't struggle to get up in the morning.
4. Prioritize what's important. Focus on the most important things and let minor things fall into place.
5. Learn to say no. You won't be able to do everything, and that's ok. Understand that something's can wait or people can do for themselves. If you always say yes to people and never take care of the things you need to, others will run your life, and you won't have control of it. You are not being mean if you have to say no to certain things and yes to yourself sometimes.
6. Take action. Once you have a plan together, you must take action to execute it. Don't be afraid to step out on faith. You never know what will come from it. But if you never step out and take action you can guarantee that nothing will happen.
7. Make sure you have accountability. Life happens to every last one of us, as we know. But having someone there to hold you accountable to your action plans helps you so much when you have those moments where you veer off. Having someone else that knows the goals you are trying to reach can hold you accountable to actually seeing that goal happen. They can help motivate you and pick you up during difficult times in your life when you get off track. We all need accountability and cannot do this alone.

Chapter 17
Conquering Your Fears

Before we begin this chapter, I want to make it very clear that not all forms of fear are bad. Proverbs 9:10 reads, "The fear of the Lord is the beginning of wisdom, and knowledge of the Holy One is understanding." Fear as we read in this scripture is referring to reverence of the Lord. This fear does not want to displease God and gladly submits to His will. This fear springs from love and causes us not to want to offend Him but to partake in things that please Him. Such a healthy fear enables us to rightly serve God with due respect and obedience to His will. The fear of the Lord we should desire because it is the foundation of true godly wisdom.

Now that we have briefly discussed the fear of God, I want to take a look at unhealthy fear that hinders us from operating according to God's will. Fear is simply an emotion we all face at some point in our lives. In fact, you are probably facing some degree of fear right now. I would even go so far as to say that fear is one of the most powerful emotions we can experience. But understand that fear is always the result of something deeper and is never the root issue in and of itself.

So why do we all deal with fear to such great levels? Let's go back to when we see the first display of fear in the Bible. In the book of Genesis, when God created Adam and Eve and placed them in the garden, He told them that they could eat of any fruit of any tree except the fruit from the Tree of the Knowledge of Good and Evil. However, the serpent that lurked around the garden deceived them into thinking they could eat of the very tree that God commanded them not to. The serpent told Adam and Eve that if they ate from the tree, they would be like God, knowing both good and evil. They believed the serpent and ate the fruit. They were in fact, already like God, made in His image, but the enemy was able to deceive Adam and Eve because they feared not knowing what good and evil was. Fear is an unpleasant emotion in the mind that arises with the awareness of approaching danger, whether it is known or unknown. Therefore, deception ignited the emotion of fear in their lives.

The second thing we see in the same Genesis passage is that after Adam and Eve became aware of good and evil, they realized they were both naked. When God called to them in the garden, they immediately ran and hid from Him. God asked Adam, "Where are you?"

"I heard you walking in the garden, so I hid. I was afraid because I was naked," Adam said.

"Who told you that you were naked?" God asked. "Did you eat from the tree I commanded you not to eat from?" (Genesis 3:9-11).

Adam and Eve were shameful of their nakedness, which caused them to hide. This time shame ignited the emotion of fear in their lives.

Just as deception and shame were the roots of fear in Adam and Eve's lives, we must also identify the root of fear in our lives. Where does your fear stem from? If you are to conquer your fears, you must begin with identifying and dealing with the root cause. Fear can masquerade itself in different forms. There is fear of failure. Fear of what is known, so you shrink back in terror. There is fear of the unknown. There's fear of making the "wrong" decision, so you just stand still and never move. Then there's fear that you mask as caution. That's where you try to spiritualize not doing something because you're terrified of the outcome. People deal with the fear of being rejected. There is also the fear of change. There is fear from traumatic experiences that literally paralyzes you. I believe we all deal with each of these fears on different levels, at some point in time. However, you do not have to live in a perpetual state of fear. Fear is one of the most crippling things in life and to your purpose that you could ever encounter because it's rooted in uncontrolled thoughts in your mind. You know how you can "think" of a situation and the emotion of fear is activated even though that situation is not really happening. You are experiencing real emotions based on how your mind and body is responding to a situation that is not happening. Basically, we "think" fear into existence.

However, It is essential for you to understand that fear is not real so you know how to conquer it. The first way to truly conquer fear is to acknowledge that it's there. I remember there was a time I was to lead my first Bible study group on a college campus. I was genuinely excited all up until the day that I was supposed to lead it. I allowed fear to cause me to shy away from leading. Now, do you remember when I said fear is not the root issue? The root of my issue was inadequacy that created fear. I didn't think that I was capable of leading a Bible study. I thought that I wouldn't do a good job and the fear of failing overwhelmed me. So I literally told myself that I was sick and I became physically ill. I started to feel lightheaded and weak, and I had to back out. I didn't go. I'm sure God would have used me to impact lives that day, but I gave into fear.

Once we can be honest with ourselves about the fact that we deal with fear on many levels, then we can begin to identify the root of where that fear is stemming from. Have you been through traumatic experiences? Is it rejection? Is it fear of the unknown? Is it inadequacy? Is it of shame and guilt? Is it of change? Is it feelings of inferiority? Is it feelings of being left out or missing out? Or is it something else? What are the uncontrolled thoughts in your MIND that are ushering fear into your existence? Since fear is never the root issue and is the result of something deeper we can say, it's a byproduct of your own feelings and thus not real. I do want to make it clear that, what you feel is very real. Your feelings and thoughts come from your subconscious mind that has been shaped over time, based off the things you've seen, heard, experienced and encountered in your life, and it has created an established set of attitudes and behaviors in your life. It's time to do some soul-searching because fear can hinder you from stepping out into the will of God for your life.

We have to tell ourselves that fear isn't real. This is a constant, everyday practice that we must do. Please believe me when I say that this is something that I have to tell myself every second of the day. If I give room to it, it will hinder me from moving forward. Likewise, the longer you allow yourself to give in to the lies of fear; you will not be able to move forward either. The fear of failure, wondering if you will fail if you dare to step out and do what God has called you to do can be a very scary thought. I understand. Each time in the Bible when God's chosen people expressed fear, God said, "Fear not for I am with you." So, we aren't the first generation of people that are experiencing fear. They experienced it back then as well, but God said I am with you and they moved forward and accomplished great things! Because they said no to fear and accomplished such amazing things, we are still benefiting from their actions today. We can still read about their many accomplishments in the Bible. A great saying I was told goes like this: "Even if you are afraid, do it anyway, do it afraid." That's what many people of the Bible had to do. They pushed past the fear and understood that God was with them. They did not allow fear to stop them, and they simply did it anyway.

We have to trust in the Lord. 2 Timothy 1:7 says, "For God has not given us the spirit of fear but of power and of love and of a sound mind." If we allow the spirit of love and peace to resonate in our hearts and our minds, it will usher out fear so that we can live a life of victorious power that God declared for us to live in the first place. We must trust God to guide our minds and our lives. If we allow God to have precedence, there is no way we will not accomplish what he set forth for us to do. Because we will not be doing it within our own selves, but we will be relying on the power of the Holy Spirit that will never fail. His love never fails, and he has given us the spirit of love as indicated in the Scripture above. It's vital that you learn how to identify the root of fear in your life. Secondly, tell yourself daily that fear is not real when it tries to present itself in your life. Lastly, learn to depend and trust in the Holy Spirit that guides our minds and our hearts and gives us the power to accomplish everything that God has set before us. We conquer fear by action so let's step out on the promises of God!

Chapter 18
Walking in Courage

In the book of Joshua 1:6, God says to Joshua, "Be strong and courageous for you are the one who will lead these people to possess all the land I swore to the ancestors I would give them; be strong and very courageous." I want to set this up for you, so you understand what's happening in this passage of Scripture. God said to Joshua three different times in this chapter to be strong and courageous. Why did He say it three different times? Because God knows the pressures at the beginning of your journey are probably higher than any other time in your life. At the beginning, when we are dealing with all the emotions of fear, pain, doubt, insecurity, and uncertainty the enemy loves to creep in and uproot what little faith we have before we see the full purpose of God fulfilled in our lives.

Moses, whom God had chosen to deliver the Israelites from Egypt, had just died and Joshua, his successor, was now expected to lead them into the Promised Land. I think it's worth noting here that Joshua walked very closely alongside Moses the entire time as Moses's right-hand man, so to speak. So he had the opportunity to see Moses in action, as well as see God in action as miracle after miracle was being performed right before his very eyes! God gave Joshua the same promise that He gave Moses, that wherever he and God's chosen people would set their feet, they would be on land that He had given them. God was telling Joshua to go ahead in strength and courage because He had already given him the land. Joshua simply had to go and possess it. Yet we see God is still telling Joshua to be strong and courageous so Joshua can possess something that is already his. It is the same with us, when God calls us, we still have to be strong and walk courageously in our lives in order to possess that which God has already given us.

Perhaps you're reading this book today, and you're thinking to yourself, "How do I walk in courage? I want to be courageous, but I just don't feel like I am." Courage is the willingness to confront uncertainty, fear, or intimidation in your life. It's having strength in the face of adversity.

You have to first understand that with the promises of God, He has already made a way for you to possess it. It is already yours! If something is not yours, you are less prone to take it, and you should be because you would then be stealing something. However, if I were to place you in a large room, where there is a large collection of items, and one of those items is yours, you are not going to ask anyone for it. Why? Because you know that it's yours. You are just going to take it because it belongs to you. You don't need permission to take something that already belongs to you. When we can truly grasp that concept and truth, regardless of what obstacles we have to face, that the thing you're trying to reach is already yours, all you have to do is walk up and grab it, you become more prone to take it.

Secondly, you have to understand that God will not fail you or abandon you. God values His name more than anything, and for the sake of His name, He will not fail. Through it all, God will be with you! It's so assuring to know that we are not stepping out on our own, but that God is with us the entire time. God cannot and will never fail so if the one who never fails is with you then neither will you fail.

Obedience is a key factor in walking in true courage. It's not always easy to be obedient when we are unsure of where the obedience will lead. However, we must know that obedience to God's word will always lead us to where God wants us to be.

God specifically told Joshua to be careful to obey all the instructions that Moses gave him. Obedience aligns you in the perfect will of God and gives you a confidence that otherwise, you may not have had on your own. For example, let's look at an exam. Nobody likes to read the instructions or directions at the top of the page. We just want to go straight into the questions and start answering them. However, those instructions give important information on how to proceed with the exam. If we do not read and obey the instructions, we are likely to fail the entire exam. Not so much because we didn't know the correct answers rather, because the answers weren't applicable to the instructions. Therefore, obedience is like a road map that will lead you exactly to where God wants you to be.

Joshua1:8 it says, "Study this book of instructions continually and meditate on it day and night so you will be sure to obey everything written in it; only then will you prosper and succeed in all you do." The word of God gives us confidence and courage to walk out a life that God has for us. When you effectively study for a test or study a subject matter of any sort, you feel more confident that you will pass the test or succeed in whatever it is you're studying because you've invested the time getting a better understanding of the material. That's because you have gained a higher level of knowledge and confidence. So, God is telling Joshua to study and know the instructions that Moses gave him. Meditate on it, or in other words, get it in your heart and your mind so that you will obey it and be successful in all you do. To walk in courage and be successful in the call of God on your life is to be obedient to His word and to align your life with what He's already commanded you to do.

Lastly, trusting in the Lord is an essential part of having confidence. You have to trust the God who called you; having absolute certainty that He will help you succeed if you follow all the instructions He has given you. Trusting in the Lord means depending on Him and not yourself, at all times and in all things. You must allow Him to lead you and order your steps. The moment you begin trusting in yourself or placing your trust in others is the moment you have begun self-sabotaging all that God has planned for your life. The Bible instructs us in Proverbs 3:5-6 to "Trust in the Lord with all your heart; do not depend on your own understanding. Seek his will in all you do, and he will show you which path to take."

Chapter 19
Strategic Connections

I define strategic connections as those connections that are made by people who are uniquely designed to help you better fulfill the purpose of God in your life. These connections are often divine in nature. They provide some type of resource or opportunity that was not previously available or as easily accessible to you before. These connections are so helpful and not everyone has them. I call them connections because not everyone you connect with along your journey will have a relationship with you and that's totally fine.

It was the winter of 2016, and I was working with a lady who had a very unique, non-profit organization. She was always scheduling meetings and having lunch with people about this particular organization. I loved connecting with people and being amid the wisdom and insight that was shared at these meetings. I remember meeting this one lady in particular at a luncheon one day who was sharing details about a retreat that she was hosting. She'd asked me to be a part of it, and excitedly I inquired about the details to see if I could make it. Once I looked at the information that was emailed, I reluctantly informed her I was not able to make it. However, I kept that information stored, not knowing I would later use that same facility. I met that lady at lunch one day not knowing that what she held in that email would turn out to be very vital to what God was doing in my life. It was the retreat facility that I had been praying and asking God about. If I had never met her that winter day, I probably would not have had those details so easily accessible otherwise. The awesome thing about the whole situation is that I never saw her again, however, she connected me to some vital information pertaining to my purpose. That is what I like to call a strategic or divine connection.

Sometimes we can get these confused because we think that every connection we make is someone who is meant to be in our lives long-term, but that's not the case. Some connections can last a lifetime, but there are some that are just meant to be purposeful during that season of life, to help usher you closer to your destiny.

In order to make any type of connections, you should seek opportunities through networking. It's harder to make any connections from your home. If I had not gone out to lunch that day, I would've never met that lady. It was an opportunity that I did not let pass by. Now, of course, I had no idea that I would meet her that day, but if I decided not to go out that day, I would have missed that opportunity, and missed something very important. That's how crucial seeking and being open to opportunities can affect us. There are opportunities all around you, but sometimes they pass you by because you're too tired or you don't feel like it. There are many reasons people miss opportunities, whether justified or not. You miss opportunities and you miss divine appointments anytime you fail to take action. So always seek opportunities to be in the presence of greatness. Always seek to be in the presence of those that you want to pattern your life after or who you look up to because you never know who you'll meet in the process. God could be positioning you to lock arms with someone that'll run with you, make way for or follow you. DON'T MISS OPPORTUNITIES FOR STRATEGIC CONNECTIONS!

Be approachable. Everyone loves a friendly face. It's like a magnet! People are drawn to those with bright, beautiful smiles and joyous personalities. We've heard it said, "A frown turns people around." But when you carry yourself with poise, it literally attracts people to you, and they want to know who you are. This is how you set yourself up to make strategic connections with people.

Make every person that you meet feel important. It's something about when a person feels special or valued they want to connect with you because you could touch something on the inside of them.

All throughout your lifetime, God will give you opportunities to strategically connect with others all around you. What I've learned in my life is that every time I fail to take action, whether because I'm afraid or because I'm being lazy and making excuses, I miss God opportunities. Perhaps it was an opportunity to attend an event that you passed up because you didn't "feel" like going? Perhaps it was an opportunity to accept a job offer that you passed up because the money wasn't right? Perhaps it was an opportunity to network with someone(s) that you passed up because they didn't perfectly mesh with your personality? The list goes on and on. God is constantly putting great opportunities before you each and every day. And I just want to ask you, are you seizing them? Are you taking advantage of them? If not, I want to encourage you to get serious about it and ask yourself, "Why am I letting God opportunities pass me by? What excuses am I making up that I'm convincing myself are legitimate as to why I'm not doing what God is calling me to do?" When you slow down long enough to really meditate on your behaviors, you will discover some truths about yourself that might be hard to accept at first. I know I did. However, it's necessary for your growth and development. You may even need to connect with someone who will "keep it real" with you. It's a lot easier for us to live in denial when it comes to our areas that need development.

Perhaps your approach to opportunities in the past has not been spiritually balanced? I'm not going to go into too much detail here on this; however, it's worth noting that sometimes we can spend too much time "praying" about something and never move on it. Eventually, that opportunity passes us by, never to come our way again. Think about Jesus. How many times did He have to pray about healing someone before He did it? He was able to quickly recognize opportunities when they came His way, and He immediately acted on them. How was He able to do this? I believe He was able to do this because He stayed in a constant state or attitude of prayer. He didn't need to fast and pray about every decision because His state of mind was always focused on the things that mattered to the Father. When your lifestyle is such that you're constantly kingdom minded, you will find it easy to make decisions. Your thoughts are no longer cloudy. You're no longer uncertain. You won't need to pray about things for weeks, only to still reach a decision that you're unsure about.

Conversely, we can spend no time at all praying about something and approach it with poor judgment, lacking the wisdom necessary for that opportunity. While God will send opportunities your way, He will always equip you with the tools needed to take full advantage of those opportunities. Said another way, God will never send opportunities your way that He has not prepared you for. I've seen great people who were able to recognize God opportunities in their lives, yet they did not pray about it first, and therefore their approach to those opportunities was incorrect, and the opportunity slipped through their fingers like sand. Recognizing a God opportunity is not enough. We must strive to be in a perpetual state of prayer, whereby we know exactly what to do when opportunities come our way. If you recognize the opportunity to be a God opportunity, but you're not sure how to approach it or what to do with it, consult other Godly friends or family members. Be careful not to add too much of your personal thoughts and feelings to the opportunity. In other words, don't ask a friend, "I have a great opportunity in front of me, but I'm not sure about it. It sounds good, but I have my reservations." They're likely to side with you and advise you to stay away from it. When you have a God opportunity in front of you that you're not sure what to do with, you must pray about what He would have you to do with that opportunity. Get Godly counsel. But whatever you do, don't let it pass you by and try to later fall back on the excuse of, "I wasn't ready." God won't send opportunities your way that you're not ready for. He knows you better than you know yourself. Seize every opportunity He sends your way because in those opportunities are strategic connections that will draw you closer to the purpose that He created you for.

Chapter 20
Leaving a Legacy

Dr. Martin Luther King, Jr., Billy Graham, Leonard Ravenhill, Malcolm X, are names that most people in America recognize today. I believe these are names that will forever go down in history as world changers. The lives that they lived made an impact during their lifetime, as well as the time after, and it will continue to make an impact on the times to come. The apostles Paul, Peter, and John all made a significant impact during their lifetime as well. What did these people do during their lives to make such an impact in the world, that they were able to leave such strong and lasting legacies?

First, let's take a look at what legacy is and then what did they do that made such an impact. Legacy is leaving something behind for the people coming after you. It's anything handed down from the past generation to the present. It's not something that happens overnight; it grows with each new experience. It's the ability to inspire others. We many times think that legacy is what happens at the end of your life however it is actually the sum of all of the decisions you've made during your life, the actions you took, and even the mistakes that you've made over the course of your life.

You must know who you are as an individual and what you stand for, first and foremost, if you want to leave a legacy behind. What are the core values that define you and guide the actions you take? Your core values do influence how you lead, and what causes you decide to stand for. Do people know the real you and what you represent as a leader? Not too long ago my mom said to me, "Lisa I don't think you know who you are." In my astonishment, "I said mom I've been operating in my purpose and doing what God has called me to do for the last 14 years, surely I know who I am". That statement shocked me, but nonetheless, it caused me to question, "Did I know who I was?" If my mom couldn't see that I knew who I was, then what is really going on? Then it dawned on me that the service work I did would never show people who I really was. Service work never equates to the core of who you are. For years I was in the public eye, yet very hidden from people. What I mean by that is for years; I did work for the kingdom of God, but the person of Lisa I did not show because I was very reserved, quiet and hidden in my emotions. I knew exactly who I was however if the people around me couldn't see who I was then what was the point of only me knowing when the whole goal is to impact the people around you? To others, I seemed to be very confused and lost because I hid myself for years. No one will ever want to follow someone who's lost and confused. I had to begin peeling back the layers of Lisa and allowing people to see who I really was so that they would know my heart and what I was passionate about.

What you are passionate about is generally what you are willing to fight for or make an impact in. What drives you? What does your heart burn for? What is it that bothers you with an uneasiness to see changed around you or in the world? What wakes you up in the mornings? I am passionate about the development of the believer. Seeing them set free, delivered from bondage and growing in maturity in Christ. Being fully equipped to reach their full potential in what God has called them to do. I see so many people that love the Lord but are bound by their past addictions or strongholds or even sin. Knowing that is not the life that God has called them to live, I am passionate about seeing the change. In fact, there have been many times when I've found myself guilty of being more passionate about seeing a change in someone's life, than the person I was trying to help was about seeing a change in his or her own life. I know that is nothing but the enemy stealing the freedom that God has already paid for in His people. So I began to disciple and work with women on how to get free and walking out freedom in their lives. My passion directed me to where I should begin making a change.

Making this kind of change is not easy. I've seen it happen before; people change and they're totally free but then they go back into a world that hasn't changed or a family that hasn't changed, and they fall under the pressure, and they're not sure how to walk it out. One thing I had to be sure about when embarking on this journey was that I understood the people that were around me and how they would be affected by this kind of change. Not everyone is accustomed to this and therefore not open to it. People fear what they don't understand, and if you have not been cultured in a particular way, you're more prone to think that your way is right. You have to understand the individual person, how they will handle this amongst the people that are closest to them, amongst the people in their church, amongst people in the workplace and so forth. When you can understand the people and what you're working with, it can give you more insight and sensitivity on how to go about the change.

Many times you start this journey off alone. It's not until you stand strong on your decision and convictions that people begin to join you. You first have to be sold on what you're going to do if you want other people to buy in. You see, there's no doubt in my mind that walking in complete freedom and deliverance is the life that God has called every believer to live. I fully understand the impact that this will make on a person's life. I used to sit around wishing that I could do something about helping women truly walk in freedom. It plagued my mind and my heart daily. Knowing the impact that Christ can make in their lives caused me to make a decision: I could either do something about it or sit back and keep praying. There's only so much praying we can do about a situation before God says, "Step out and do it." If we only just continue to sit back and pray, nothing will ever happen. God works through people. God has equipped us to be His hands and feet on the earth. So often, God will say, "I'm waiting on you to act."

We have to have enough courage to do it even if nobody understands it, or if we are alone for a while. Stepping out in faith for what God has called you to do definitely takes courage. Even when all odds seem to be against you, it's okay, if you know it will make an impact. We have to be willing to take a calculated risk and have a well thought out plan. We never really set out knowing how great of an impact we are going to make: only that we will make an impact. That's the thing about legacy; it carries on from generation to generation, to generation. That's why it's so important for us not to be afraid to step out in faith and take a risk and do what God has put on our hearts. You never know the impact that it will make. I'm sure Dr. Martin Luther King, Jr. was just tired of the injustice, so he took a stand, and he did something about it, not knowing how great of an impact that he would make. Not knowing that decades later, he would still be talked about and have his own day in remembrance of him. We have to be willing to step out and do the same.

Chapter 21
Commitment

I intentionally placed this chapter on commitment at the end of this book because I believe this is the most important chapter. You see, people generally pay attention to the first and the last thing they hear, read, or see. I wanted to make sure that the last message you take away from this book would be the most life-changing message. Let's talk about a few areas that we should be committed to, as we draw close to the end of this book.

Commitment is everything! I'm sure you've noticed how each chapter in this book has built upon the previous chapter and has consistently introduced new levels of freedom in your life! However, if you are not committed to the Lord and seeing your purpose come to pass, it simply won't happen. Commitment is the bridge that allows you to successfully pass from one point in your life to the next. Simply put, it's the state of being dedicated or devoted to someone or a worthy cause.

Many of us will argue that we are committed people, and I would actually have to agree with that claim. When you look at your life, it's clear that you are committed to various things in so many ways. It takes commitment to get up each day and go to work at the same time every day. You are devoted to making sure that you keep your job. Perhaps you do this every day because you need the money. Perhaps you genuinely enjoy what you do. No matter what the reason is, there is a level of commitment and faithfulness that compels you to keep doing it.

Think about someone you may know, whether personally or indirectly, who loves sport. Perhaps that person is you. That person is so committed to their sport of choice that there is absolutely no way they will ever miss a game. And please don't ask them to do something during game time. Being committed to something can even include things such as watching favorite TV shows. I can remember a time in my life when if you asked me to do anything on a Tuesday night at seven o'clock pm, it was an automatic, "No," because I knew that The Flash was coming on and I didn't want to miss it. I was literally dedicated to watching that show when it first aired and not a second later. I can go down the list of the endless possibilities of things that every individual would say they are committed to. I believe that every person is committed to something or someone so it's not a matter of are you committed, I believe the deeper, more important question you should ask yourself today is, "What am I committed to?"

We are to be committed to the Lord our God. As mentioned, we can be committed to so many things, but the Lord requires us to be committed to Him first and foremost. Many people say they are committed to the Lord, but their lives generally show what they are genuinely committed to. Think about the people who will get up every day and go to work, but on Sunday's, church is optional for them. Yet they consider themselves to be committed to the Lord. Why is this? I believe it's because of their commitment level to serving the Lord. I don't share this example to pass judgment. I simply share it to prove the point that when we are truly committed to something or someone, our words and actions will bear witness to the truth of that fact. I understand that going to church doesn't completely measure a person's level of commitment to the Lord. I agree that one should assess his or her own prayer and devotional life, in addition to their involvement in their local church. However, it's been my experience that most people who have a hard time going to church once a week, have an even harder time reading the Bible and praying regularly.

When I was a freshman in college in Baton Rouge, Louisiana, I had a job working at Chick-fil-A. I had to work on one of the worst days in a college student's life, at the worst time imaginable. Somehow, I was stuck with the Saturday morning, six o'clock AM shift. That's right, I had to be at work for six o'clock AM on a Saturday morning, which meant I had to get up even earlier to get ready and be on the road to make it on time. At that point in my life, I didn't even know I could get up that early and be somewhere on a Saturday morning. However, I never missed a day. During that same time, the Lord would ask me to get up at six o'clock AM to pray daily before I started my day for class. I made every excuse in the book on why it was so hard for me to get up at six to read and pray. Then the Lord began to show me that if I can get up on a Saturday morning to get ready for a job, surely I could get up daily to spend time with Him. This hit me very hard. It forced me to begin to really think about why this was the case. My commitment to not losing my job and having that form of income was more important to me than growing in my relationship with the Lord. If you were, to be honest with yourself, would you say that this describes you? Are you able to make arrangements for other people or things, even to the point of getting out of your comfort zone, but when it comes to the things of God, you find it difficult to be committed? What you are committed to is what you will pursue or allow to take up residence in your life. I can say all day that my relationship with the Lord is more important to me than anything else in life, but if my actions don't show that, then it's not true. We say all the time, "I love the Lord! He is the most important thing to me." But then we slack on our commitment to serving Him and reading His word, or even praying to Him without interruptions.

If your commitment to the Lord is not as strong as you would like it to be today, be encouraged because I specifically wrote this book to inspire and help you to make that change so that you will be wholeheartedly devoted to serving the Lord. Being committed to the Lord is not lip service; it's a life service. How is it that we can read books upon books but not read His book? If we have time to read then we have to ask ourselves why isn't the word of God priority in my life? Relationships have always been and are still very important to me. There was a time in my life that I wanted to make sure that every relationship in my life was in good standing. I mean I fought hard to get out all the kinks and make sure that there were no issues in my relationships. It began to consume me at one point. In pursuit of making a relationship right, the Lord spoke to me and said, "I wish you were that concerned about your relationship with me." This may be the case for you as well. Like I was, you might be more committed to people than you are to the Lord right now. But the Lord wants to be the Lord of your life. He desires to be at the very center of your life.

We have to be committed to reading and living by the word of God. Many people seek to do this by reading devotionals. There is absolutely nothing wrong with devotionals; however, a devotional is someone else laying out what they have learned during their time with the Lord. We are reading their rhema word from the Bible. It's always better when we pick up the word of God ourselves and allow the Lord to speak to us directly. I challenge you not only to read a devotional but to crack open the Bible for yourself. God wants us to dig into His word and allow it to transform every part of our mind, body, and soul. You have to be committed to the things of God more than you are to anything else if you are going to truly allow the Lord to move in your life and fulfill the purpose that He's given you. Don't get me wrong; I never liked getting up early on a Saturday morning to have to be at work for six. But the more I did it, the easier it became. The same was true when I first started reading the word of God. I didn't fully understand everything I was reading, but the more I read it, the more I wanted to read it, the more I wanted to learn, the more I wanted it to change me.

"If you love me, obey my commandments," Jesus said in John 14:15. This scripture is pretty straightforward; we have to be committed to obeying God's word. I know that's so much easier said than done. Commitment stems from the level of love that you have in your heart for a person or a thing. That's really what it all boils down to. If you love someone, you will want to be committed to him or her. If you love something, you want to go all out for it. Don't be found being more committed to people than you are to the Lord.

If you want to fulfill your God-given purpose in life, you will have to be committed to your local church, your prayer time, as well as your time in God's word. It is almost impossible to fulfill your God-given mission outside of your connection to the local church. Church should not be optional for you. Two-thirds of the New Testament in the Bible was written to the believers in the church. Those books were not written to standalone Christians or people who were not connected to the Lord's body. The church is the hope of the world! Jesus is coming back for his bride, which is the church. He told Peter, "Upon this rock, I will build my church, and the gates of hell shall not prevail against it."-Matthew 16:18. Christ gave His life for the church, that's how important it is. Our commitment to serving and being connected to our local church should be greater than our commitment to doing life alone.

I also believe that we should be committed to influential figures in our life such as pastors, leaders, mentors and even those we value and trust within our family. They can offer great wisdom and insight. However Jesus says that our commitment to Him must supersede our commitment to even those we value most. The reason for this is because the trials and tribulations we may endure in life, everyone may not understand. The call of God on your life should come before anything or anyone, for it is the will of God. Sometimes the things the Lord will require of you or the places the Lord will require you to go may not line up with what other people think is right for you, but your allegiance to being obedient to the Lord has to be greater than the opinions of even those closest to you. By no means am I saying to ignore what they have to say to you. I actually had to learn that the hard way. The Lord opened my understanding to being receptive to my family because there was a time when I did not heed to their wisdom. I found myself in a series of bad decisions because of it. But what I'm saying is, take all wisdom into consideration, and at the end of the day, be committed to going forward and doing what the Lord has called you to do even if people don't understand it. God has called you; therefore go forth!

Made in the
USA
Lexington, KY